Clay's Ark

CLAY'S ARK

Octavia E. Butler

St. Martin's Press
New York

Design by Lee Wade

Library of Congress Cataloging in Publication Data

Butler, Octavia E.
  Clay's ark.

  I. Title.
PS3552.U827C55 1984   813'.54   83-17766
ISBN 0-312-14321-4

10 9 8 7 6 5 4 3 2

In memory of Phyllis White

PART 1

PHYSICIAN

PAST 1

The ship had been destroyed five days before. He did not remember how. He knew he was alone now, knew he had returned home instead of to the station as planned or to the emergency base on Luna. He knew it was night. For long stretches of time, he knew nothing else.

He walked and climbed automatically, hardly seeing the sand, the rock, the mountains, noticing only those plants that could be useful to him. Hunger and thirst kept him moving. If he did not find water soon, he would die.

He had hidden for five days and two nights, had wandered for nearly three nights with no destination, no goal but food, water, and human companionship. During this time he killed jack rabbits, snakes, even a coyote, with his bare hands or with stones. These he ate raw, splashing their blood over his ragged coverall, drinking as much of it as he could. But he had found little water.

Now he could smell water the way a dog or a horse might. This was no longer a new sensation. He had become accustomed to using his senses in ways not normally thought human. In his own mind, his humanity had been in question for some time.

He walked. When he reached rocks at the base of a range of mountains, he began to climb, rousing to notice the change only because moving began to require more effort, more of his slowly fading strength.

For a few moments, he was alert, sensitive to the rough, eroded granite beneath his hands and feet, aware that there were people in the direction he had chosen. This was not surprising. On the desert, people would either congregate around water or bring water with them. On one level, he was eager to join them. He needed the company of other people almost as badly as he needed water. On another level, he hoped the people would be gone from the water when he reached it. He was able to distinguish the smell of women among them, and he began to sweat. He hoped at least that the women would be gone. If they stayed, if anyone stayed, they risked death. Some of them would surely die.

PRESENT 2

The wind had begun to blow before Blake Maslin left Needles on his way west toward Palos Verdes Enclave and home. City man that he was, Blake did not worry about the weather. His daughter Keira warned him that desert winds could blow cars off the road and that wind-driven sand could blast paint off cars, but he reassured her. He had gotten into the habit of reassuring her without really listening to her fears; there were so many of them.

This time, however, Keira was right. She should have been. The desert had long been an interest of hers, and she knew it better than Blake did. This whole old-fashioned car trip had happened because she knew and loved the desert—and because she wanted to see her grandparents—Blake's parents—in Flagstaff, Arizona, one last time. She wanted to visit them in the flesh, not just see them on a phone screen. She wanted to be with them while she was still well enough to enjoy them.

Twenty minutes out of Needles, the wind became a gale. There were heavy, billowing clouds ahead, black and gray slashed by lightning, but there was no rain yet. Nothing to hold down the dust and sand.

For a while Blake tried to continue on. In the back seat, Keira slept, breathing deeply, almost snoring. It bothered him when he could no longer hear her over the buffeting of the wind.

His first-born daughter, Rane, sat beside him, smiling slightly, watching the storm. While he fought to control the car, she enjoyed herself. If Keira had too many fears, Rane had too few. She and Keira were fraternal twins, different in appearance and behavior. Somehow, Blake had slipped into the habit of thinking of the hardier, more impulsive Rane as his younger daughter.

A gust of wind slammed into the car broadside, almost blowing it off the road. For several seconds, Blake could see nothing ahead except a wall of pale dust and sand.

Frightened at last, he pulled off the road. His armored, high-suspension Jeep Wagoneer was a hobby, a carefully preserved relic of an earlier, oil-extravagant era. It had once run on one-hundred-percent gasoline, though now it used ethanol. It was bigger and heavier than the few other cars on the road, and Blake was a good driver. But enough was enough—especially with the girls in the car.

When he was safely stopped, he looked around, saw that other people were stopping too. On the other side of the highway, ghostly in the blowing dust and sand, were three large trucks— expensive private haulers, carrying God-knew-what: anything, from the household possessions of the wealthy, who could still afford the archaic luxury of moving across country, to the necessities of the few remaining desert enclaves and roadside stations, to illegal drugs, weapons, and worse. Several yards ahead, there was a battered Chevrolet and a new little electric something-or-other. Far behind, he could see another private hauler parked at such a strange angle that he knew it had come off the highway barely under control. Only a few thrillseekers in aging tour buses continued on.

From out of the desert over a dirt road Blake had not previously noticed came another car, making its way toward the highway. Blake stared at it, wondering where it could have come from. This part of the highway was bordered on both sides by some of the bleakest desert Blake had ever seen—worn volcanic hills and emptiness.

Incongruously, the car was a beautiful, old, wine-red Mercedes—the last thing Blake would have expected to see coming out of the wilderness. It drove past him on the sand, traveling east, though the only lanes open to it carried westbound traffic. Blake wondered whether the driver would be foolish enough to try to cross the highway in the storm. He could see three people in the car as it passed but could not tell whether they were men or women. He watched them disappear into the dust behind him, then forgot them as Keira moaned in her sleep.

He looked at her, felt rather than saw that Rane also turned to look. Keira, thin and frail, slept on.

"Back in Needles," Rane said, "I heard a couple of guys talking about her. They thought she was so pretty and fragile."

Blake nodded. "I heard them too." He shook his head. Keira had been pretty once—when she was healthy, when she looked so much like her mother that it hurt him. Now she was ethereal, not quite of this world, people said. She was only sixteen, but she had acute myeloblastic leukemia—an adult disease—and she was not responding to treatment. She wore a wig because the epigenetic therapy that should have caused her AML cells to return to normal had not worked, and her doctor, in desperation, had resorted to old-fashioned chemotherapy. This had caused most of her hair to fall out. She had lost so much weight that none of her clothing fit her properly. She said she could see herself fading away. Blake could see her fading, too. As an internist, he could not help seeing more than he wanted to see.

He looked away from Keira and out of the corner of his eye he saw something bright green move at Rane's window. Before he could speak, a man who seemed to come from nowhere tore open her door, *which had been locked,* and moved to shove his way in beside Rane.

The man was quick, and stronger than any two men should

have been, but he was also slightly built and off-balance. Before he could regain his balance, Rane screamed an obscenity, drew her legs back against her body, and spring-released them so that they slammed into his abdomen.

The man doubled and fell backward onto the ground, his green shirt flapping in the wind. Instantly another man took his place. The second man had a gun.

Frightened, Rane drew back against Blake, and Blake, who had reached for his own automatic rifle sheathed diagonally on the door next to him, froze, staring at the intruder's gun. It was not aimed at him. It was aimed at Rane.

Blake raised his hands, held them in midair, clearly empty. For a long moment, he could not speak. He could only stare at the short, dull black carbine leveled at his daughter.

"You can have my wallet," he said finally. "It's in my pocket."

The man seemed to ignore him.

The red Mercedes pulled up beside Blake's car and Blake could see that there was only one person inside now. A woman, he thought. He could see what looked like a great deal of long, dark hair.

The man in the green shirt picked himself up and drew a handgun. Now there were two guns, both aimed at Rane. Thug psychologists. The green-shirted one walked around the car toward Blake's side.

"Touch the lock," the remaining one ordered. "Just the lock. Let him in."

Blake obeyed, let Green Shirt open the door and take the rifle. Then, in an inhumanly swift move, the man reached across Blake and ripped out the phone. "City rich!" he muttered contemptuously as Blake realized what he had done. "City slow and stupid. Now take out the wallet and give it to me."

Blake handed his wallet to Green Shirt, moving slowly, watching the guns. Green Shirt snatched the wallet, slammed the door, and went back to the other side where the two cars together offered some protection from the wind. There, he opened the wallet. Surprisingly, he did not check the cash compartment, though Blake actually had over two thousand dollars. He liked to carry small amounts of cash when he traveled. Green Shirt flipped through Blake's computer cards, pulled out his Palos Verdes Enclave identification.

"Doctor," he said. "How about that. Blake Jason Maslin, M.D. Know anybody who needs a doctor, Eli?"

The other gunman gave a humorless laugh. He was a tall, thin black man with skin that had gone gray with more than desert dust. His health may have been better than Keira's, Blake thought, but not by much.

For that matter, Green Shirt, shorter and smaller-boned, did not look healthy himself. He was blond, tanned beneath his coating of dust, though his tan seemed oddly gray. He was balding. His gun shook slightly in his hand. A sick man. They were both sick—sick and dangerous.

Blake put his arm around Rane protectively. Thank God Keira had managed to sleep through everything so far.

"What is this, anyway?" Eli demanded, glancing back at Keira, then staring at Rane. "What kind of cradles have you been robbing, Doc?"

Blake stiffened, felt Rane stiffen against him. His wife Jorah had been black, and he and Rane and Keira had been through this routine before.

"These are my daughters," Blake said coldly. Without the guns, he would have said more. Without his hand gripping Rane's shoulder, she would have said much more.

Eli looked surprised, then nodded, accepting. Most people took longer to believe. "Okay," he said. "Get out here, girl."

Rane did not move, could not have if she had wanted to. Blake held her where she was. "Dad?" she whispered.

"You have my money," Blake told Eli. "You can have anything else you want. But let my daughters alone!"

Green Shirt glanced into the back seat at Keira. "I think that one's dead," he said casually. This was supposed to be a joke about Keira's sound sleeping, Blake knew, but he could not prevent himself from looking back at her quickly—just to be sure.

"Hey, Eli," Green Shirt said, "they really are his kids, you know."

"I can see," Eli said. "And that makes our lives easier. All we have to do is take one of them and he's ours."

It was beginning to rain—fat, dirty, wind-whipped drops. In the distance, thunder rumbled over the howl of the wind.

Eli spoke so softly to Rane that Blake was hardly able to hear. "Is he your father?"

"You just admitted he was," Rane said. "What the hell do you want?"

Eli frowned. "My mother always used to say 'Think before you speak.' Your mother ever say anything like that to you, girl?"

Rane looked away, silent.

"Is he your father?" Eli repeated.

"Yes."

"And you wouldn't want to see him get hurt, would you?"

Rane continued to look away, but could not conceal her fear. "What do you want?"

Ignoring her, Eli held his hand out to Green Shirt. After a moment, Green Shirt gave him the wallet. "Blake Jason Maslin," he read. "Born seven-four-seventy-seven. 'Oh say can you see.' " He looked at Rane. "What's your name, baby?"

Rane hesitated, no doubt repelled by the casual "baby." Normally she tore into people who seemed to be patronizing her. "Rane," she muttered finally. Thunder all but drowned her out.

"Rain? Like this dirty stuff falling on us now?"

"Not rain, Rah-ney. It's Norwegian."

"Is it now? Well, listen, Rane, you see that woman over there?" He pointed to the red Mercedes alongside them. "Her name is Meda Boyd. She's crazy as hell, but she won't hurt you. And if you do what we tell you and don't give us trouble, we won't hurt your father or your sister. You understand?"

Rane nodded, but Eli continued to look at her, waiting.

"I understand!" she said. "What do you want me to do?"

"Go get in that car with Meda. She'll drive you. I'll follow with your father."

Rane looked at Blake. He could feel her trembling. "Listen," he began, "you can't do this! You can't just—"

Green Shirt placed his gun against Rane's temple. "Why not?" he asked.

Blake jerked Rane away. It was a reflex, a chance he would never have taken if he had had time to think about it. He pulled her head down against his chest.

At the same moment, Eli pulled Green Shirt's gun hand away, twisting it so that if the gun had gone off, the bullet would have hit the windshield.

The gun did not go off. It should have, Blake realized later, considering Green Shirt's tremor and the suddenness of Eli's move. But all that happened was some sort of brief, wordless exchange between Eli and Green Shirt. They looked at each other —first with real anger, then with understanding and a certain amount of sheepishness.

"You'd better drive," Eli said. "Let Meda watch the kid."

"Yeah," Green Shirt agreed. "The past catches up with you sometimes."

"You okay?"

"Yeah."

"She's a strong girl. Good material."

"I know."

"Good material for what?" Blake demanded. He had released Rane, but she stayed close to him, watching Eli.

"Look, Doc," Eli said, "the last thing we want to have to do is kill one of you. But we don't have much time or patience."

"Let my daughters stay with me," Blake said. "I'll cooperate. I'll do anything you want. Just don't—"

"We're leaving you one. Don't make us take them both."

"But—"

"Ingraham, get the other kid out here. Get her up."

"No!" Blake shouted. "Please, she's sick. Let her alone!"

"What? Carsick?"

"My sister has leukemia," Rane said. "She's dying. What are you going to do? Help her along?"

"Rane, for God's sake!" Blake whispered.

Eli and the green-shirted Ingraham looked at each other, then back at Blake. "I thought they could cure that now," Eli said. "Don't they have some kind of protein medicine that reprograms the cells?"

Blake hesitated, wondering how much pity the details of Keira's illness might evoke in the gunmen. He was surprised that Eli knew as much as he did about epigenetic therapy. But Eli's knowledge did not matter. If he was not moved by Keira's imminent death, nothing else was likely to touch them. "She's receiving therapy," he said.

"And it isn't enough?" Ingraham asked.

Blake shrugged. It hurt to say the words. He could not recall ever having said them aloud.

"Shit." Ingraham muttered. "What are we supposed to do with a kid who's already—"

"Shut up," Eli said. "If we've made a mistake, it's too late to cry about it." He glanced back at Keira, then faced Blake. "Sorry, Doc. Her bad luck and ours." He sighed. "Well, you take the good with the bad. We won't hurt her—if you and Rane do as you're told."

"What are you going to do with us?" Blake asked.

"Don't worry about it. Come on, Rane. Meda's waiting."

Rane clung to Blake as she had not for years.

Eli gazed at her steadily, and she stared back but would not move. "Come on, kid," he said softly. "Do it the easy way."

Blake wanted to tell her to go—before these people hurt her. Yet the last thing he wanted her to do was leave him. He was terrified that if they took her, he would never get her back. He stared at the two men. If he had had his gun, he would have shot them without a thought.

"Use your head, Doc," Eli said. "Just slide over to the passenger side. I'll drive. You keep your eyes on Rane. It will make you feel better. Make you act better, too."

Abruptly, Blake gave in, moved over, pushing Rane. He wanted to believe the gray-skinned black man. It would have been easier to believe him if Blake had had some idea what these people wanted. They were not just one of the local car gangs, obscenely called car families. No one had looked at the money in his wallet. In fact, as he thought about the wallet, Eli tossed it onto the dashboard as though he were finished with it. Were they after more money? Ransom? They did not sound as though they were. And they seemed strangely resigned, as though they did not like what they were doing—almost as though they were under the gun themselves.

Blake hugged Rane. "Watch yourself," he said, trying to sound steadier than he felt. "Be more careful than you usually are —at least until we find out what's going on."

Blake watched Ingraham follow Rane through the muddy downpour, watched her get into the red Mercedes. Ingraham said a few words to the woman, Meda, then exchanged places with her.

When that was done, Eli relaxed. He thrust his gun into his jacket, walked around the Wagoneer as casually as an old friend, and got in. It never occurred to Blake to try anything. Part of himself had walked away with Rane. His stomach churned with anger, frustration, and worry.

After a moment of spinning its wheels, the Mercedes leaped forward, shot all the way across the highway, and onto another dirt road. The Wagoneer followed easily. Eli patted its dashboard as though it were alive. "Sweet-running car," he said. "Big. You don't find them this size any more. Too bad."

"Too bad?"

"Strongest-looking car we saw parked along the highway. We didn't want some piece of junk that would stall or get stuck on us. One tank full and the other nearly full of ethanol. Damn good. We make ethanol."

"You mean it was my car you wanted?"

"We wanted a decent car with two or three healthy, fairly young people in it." He glanced back at Keira. "You can't win 'em all."

"But why?"

"Doc, what's the kid's name?" He jerked a thumb over his shoulder at Keira.

Blake stared at him.

"Tell her she can get up. She's been awake since Ingraham took your wallet."

Blake turned sharply, found himself looking into Keira's large, frightened eyes. He tried to calm himself for her sake. "Do you feel all right?" he asked.

She nodded, probably lying.

"Sit up," he said. "Do you know what's happened?"

Another nod. If Rane talked too much, Keira didn't talk enough. Even before her illness became apparent, she had been a timid girl, easily frightened, easily intimidated, apparently slow. Patience and observation revealed her intelligence, but most people wasted neither on her.

She sat up slowly, staring at Eli. His coloring was as bad as her own. She could not have helped noticing that, but she said nothing.

"You get an earful?" Eli asked her.

She drew as far away from him as she could get and did not answer.

"You know your sister's in that car up ahead with some friends of mine. You think about that."

"She's no danger to you," Blake said angrily.

"Have her give you whatever she's got in her left hand."

Blake frowned, looked toward Keira's left hand. She was wearing a long, multicolored, cotton caftan—a full, flowing garment with long, voluminous sleeves. It was intended to conceal her painfully thin body. At the moment, it also concealed her left hand.

Keira's expression froze into something ugly and determined.

"Kerry," Blake whispered.

She blinked, glanced at him, finally brought her left hand out of the folds of her dress and handed him the large manual screwdriver she had been concealing. Blake could remember misplacing the old screwdriver and not having time to look for it. It looked too large for Keira's thin fingers. Blake doubted that she had the strength to do any harm with it. With a smaller, sharper instrument, however, she might have been dangerous. Anyone who could look the way she did now could be dangerous, sick or well.

Blake took the screwdriver from her hand and held on to the hand for a moment. He wanted to reassure her, calm her, but he thought of Rane alone in the car ahead, and no words would come. There was no way everything was going to be all right. And he had always found it difficult to lie to his children.

After a moment, Keira seemed to relax—or at least to give up. She leaned back bonelessly, let her gaze flicker from Eli to the car ahead. Only her eyes seemed alive.

"What do you want with us?" she whispered. "Why are you doing this?" Blake did not think Eli had heard her over the buffeting of the wind and the hissing patter of the rain. Eli obviously had all he could do to keep the car on the dirt road and the Mercedes in sight. He ignored completely the long, potentially deadly screwdriver Blake gripped briefly, then dropped. He was a young man, Blake realized—in his early thirties, perhaps. He looked older—or had looked older before Blake got a close look at him. His face was thin and prematurely lined beneath its coating of dust. His air of weary resignation suggested an older man. He looked older, Blake thought, in much the same way Keira looked older. Her disease had aged her, as apparently his had aged him—whatever his was.

Eli glanced at Keira through the rearview mirror. "Girl," he said, "you won't believe me, but I wish to hell I could let you go."

"Why can't you?" she asked.

"Same reason you can't get rid of your leukemia just by wishing."

Blake frowned. That answer couldn't have made any more sense to Keira than it did to him, but she responded to it. She gave Eli a long thoughtful look and moved slowly toward the middle of the seat away from her place of retreat behind Blake.

"Do you hurt?" she asked.

He turned to look back at her—actually slowed down and lost sight of the Mercedes for a moment. Then he was occupied with catching up and there was only the sound of the rain as it was whipped against the car.

"In a way," Eli answered finally. "Sometimes. How about you?"

Keira hesitated, nodded.

Blake started to speak, then stopped himself. He did not like the understanding that seemed to be growing between his daughter and this man, but Eli, in his dispute with Ingraham, had already demonstrated his value.

"Keira," Eli muttered. "Where did you ever get a name like that?"

"Mom didn't want us to have names that sounded like everybody's."

"She saw to that. Your mother living?"

". . .no."

Eli gave Blake a surprisingly sympathetic look. "Didn't think so." There was another long pause. "How old are you?"

"Sixteen."

"That all? Are you the oldest or the youngest?"

"Rane and I are twins."

A startled glance. "Well, I guess you're not lying about it, but the two of you barely look like members of the same family —let alone twins."

"I know."

"You got a nickname?"

"Kerry."

"Oh yeah. That's better. Listen, Kerry, nobody at the ranch is going to hurt you; I promise you that. Anybody bothers you, you call me. Okay?"

"What about my father and sister?"

Eli shook his head. "I can't work no miracles, girl."

Blake stared at him, but for once, Eli refused to notice. He kept his eyes on the road.

PAST 3

In a high valley surrounded by stark, naked granite weathered round and deceptively smooth-looking, he found a finished house of wood on a stone foundation and the skeletal beginnings of two other houses. There was also a well with a huge, upended metal tank. There were pigs in wood-fenced pens, chickens in coops, rabbits in hutches, a large fenced garden, and a solar still. The still and electricity produced by photovoltaic intensifiers appeared to be the only concessions to modernity the owners of the little homestead had made.

He went to the well, turned the faucet handle of the storage tank, caught the cold, sweet, clear water in his hands, and drank. He had not tasted such water in years. It restored thought, cleared the fog from his mind. Now the senses that had been totally focused on survival were freed to notice other things.

The women, for instance.

He had scented at least one man in the house, but there were several women. Their scents attracted him powerfully. Yet the moment he caught himself moving toward the house in response to that attraction, he began to resist.

For several minutes he stood frozen outside the window of one of the women. He was so close to her he could hear her soft, even breathing. She was asleep, but turning restlessly now and then. He literally could not move. His body demanded that he go to the woman. He understood the demand, the drive, but he refused to be just an animal governed by instinct. The woman was as near to being in heat as a female human could be. She had reached the most fertile period of her monthly cycle. It was no wonder she was sleeping so badly. And no wonder he could not move except to go to her.

He stood where he was, perspiring heavily in the cold night air and struggling to remember that he had resolved to be human plus, not human minus. He was not an animal, not a rapist, not a murderer. Yet he knew that if he let himself be drawn to the woman, he would rape her. If he raped her, if he touched her at all, she might die. He had watched it happen before, and it had driven him to want to die, to try to die himself. He had tried, but he could not deliberately kill himself. He had an unconscious will to survive that transcended any conscious desire, any guilt, any duty to those who had once been his fellow humans.

He tried furiously to convince himself that a break-in and rape would be stupidly self-destructive, but his body was locked into another reality, focused on a more fundamental form of survival. He did not move until the war within had exhausted him, until he had no strength left to take the woman.

Finally, triumphant, he dragged himself back to the well and drank again. The electric pump beside the well switched on suddenly, noisily, and in the distance, dogs began to bark. He looked around, knowing from the sound that the dogs were coming toward him. He had already discovered that dogs disliked him, and, rightly enough, feared him. Now, however, he had been weakened by days of hunger and thirst and by his own internal conflict. Two or three large dogs might be able to bring him down and tear him apart.

The dogs came bounding up—two big mongrels, barking and growling. They were put off by his strange scent at first, and they kept back out of his reach while putting on a show of ferocity. He thought by the time they found the courage to attack, he might be ready for at least one of them.

PRESENT 4

Eventually, the Mercedes and the Jeep emerged from the storm into vast, flat, dry desert, still following their arrow-straight dirt road. They approached, then passed between ancient black and red volcanic mountains. Later, they turned sharply from their dirt road onto something that was little more than a poorly marked trail. This led to a range of earth and granite mountains. The two cars headed into the mountains and began winding their way upward.

By then they had been driving for nearly an hour. At first, Blake had seen a few signs of humanity. A small airport, a lonely ranch here and there, many steel towers carrying high voltage lines from the Hidalgo and Joshua Tree Solar Power Plants. (The water shortage had hurt desert settlement even as the desert sun began to be used to combat the fuel shortage. Over much of the desert, communities were dead or dying.) But for some time now, Blake had seen no sign at all that there were other people in the world. It was as though they had left 2021 and gone back in time to primordial desert. The Indians must have seen the land this way.

Blake wondered whether he and his daughters would die in this empty place. It occurred to him that his abductors might be more likely to feel they needed him if they thought of him as their doctor. They might even give him enough of an opening to take his daughters and escape.

"Look," he said to Eli, "you're obviously not well. Neither is your friend Ingraham. I have my bag with me. Maybe I can help."

"You can't help, Doc," Eli said.

"You don't know that."

"Assume that I do." Eli squeezed the car around another of a series of boulders that seemed to have been scattered deliberately along the narrow mountain road. "Assume that I'm at least as complex a man as you are."

Blake stared at him, noting with interest that Eli had dropped the easy, old-fashioned street rhythms that made his speech seem familiar and made him seem no more than another semieducated product of city sewers. If he wished, then, he could speak flat, standard, correct American English.

"What's the matter with you, then?" Blake asked. "Will you tell us?"

"Not yet."

"Why?"

Eli took his time answering. He smiled finally—a smile full of teeth and utterly without humor. "It was a group decision," he said. "We got together and decided that for your sake and ours, people in your position should be protected from too much truth too soon. I was a minority of one, voting for honesty. I could have been a majority of one, but I've played that role long enough. The others thought people like you wouldn't believe the truth, that it would scare you more than necessary and you'd try harder to escape."

To the surprise of both men, Keira laughed. Blake looked back at her, and she fell silent, embarrassed. "I'm sorry," she whispered, "but not knowing is worse. Do they really think we wouldn't do just about anything to get away now?"

"Nothing to be sorry for, girl," Eli said. The accent was back. "I agree with you."

"Who are the others who disagreed?" Keira asked.

"People. Just people like you and your father. Meda's family owned the land we live on. Ingraham . . . well, he was with a gang of bikers that came calling one day and tried to rape Meda—among other things. And we have a private hauler and a music student from L.A., a couple of people from Victorville, one from Twentynine Palms, and a few others."

"Ingraham tried to rape someone, and you let him stay?" Blake demanded. He was suddenly glad Ingraham was driving the car ahead. At least he would not have time to try anything until they got where they were going—but what then?

"That was another life," Eli said. "We don't care what he did before. He's one of us now."

Blake thought of Ingraham's gun against Rane's head.

Eli seemed to read his thoughts. "Hey," he said, "I know how it looked, but Ingraham wouldn't have shot her. I was afraid you or she might make a dumb move and cause an accident, but there's no way he would have shot her."

"Was the gun empty?" Keira asked.

"Hell no," Eli said, surprised. He hesitated. "Listen, I'll be this straight with you. The safest person of the three of you is Rane. She's young, she's female, and she's healthy. If only one of you makes it, chances are it will be her." He slowed, looked at Blake, then at Keira. "What I'm trying to do is build a fire under you two. I want you to use your minds and your plain damn stubbornness to make a liar of me. I want you all to survive." He stopped the car. "We're here."

"Here" was a small high valley—a little space between the ancient rocks that formed the mountains. There was a large old house of wood and stone and three other wooden houses, less well built. A fifth house was under construction. Two men worked on it with hand tools, hammering and sawing as almost no one did these days.

"Population explosion," Eli said. "We've been lucky lately."

"You mean people have been surviving whatever it is you do to them here?" Blake asked.

"That's what I mean," Eli admitted. "We're learning to help them."

"Are you some kind of . . . well, some kind of religious group?" Keira asked. "I don't mean any offence, but I've heard there were . . . groups in the mountains."

"Cultists?" Eli said, smiling a real smile. "No, we didn't come up here to worship anybody, girl. There were some religious people up here once, though. Not cultists, just . . . What do you call them? People who never saw sweet reason around the turn of the century, and who decided to make a decent, moral, God-fearing place of their own to raise their kids and wait for the Second Coming."

"Leftovers," Blake said. "At least that's what we called such people when I was younger. But this place looks as though it hasn't been touched by this century or the last one. Looks more like a holdover from the nineteenth."

"Yeah," Eli said, and smiled again. "Get out, Doc. Let's see if I can talk Meda into cooking you folks a meal." He took the keys, then waited until Blake and Keira got out. Then he locked their doors and got out himself.

Blake looked around and decided that almost everything he saw reminded him of descriptions he'd read of subsistence farming more than a century before. Chickens running around loose, pecking at the sand, others in coops and in a large chicken house and yard. Hogs poking their snouts between the wooden planks of their pens, rabbits in wood-and-wire hutches, a couple of cows. But every building was topped by photovoltaic intensifiers. The well had an electric pump—clearly an antique—and on the front porch of one of the houses, a woman was using an ancient black Singer sewing machine. There was a large garden growing over perhaps half the valley floor. And near the two most distant houses were small structures that might have been, of all things, outhouses.

Blake had turned to ask Eli about it when suddenly, Rane was in his arms. He hugged her, startled that even this strange place had made him forget her danger for a moment. Now, flanked by both his daughters, he felt better, stronger. The feeling was irrational, he knew. The girls were no safer for their being with him. Their captors still had the guns. And they were all still trapped in this isolated, atavistic place. Worst of all, something was being planned for them—something they might not survive.

"What did you hear?" he asked Rane while Eli was busy talking to Meda.

"I think they're on some weird drugs or something," Rane whispered. "That guy Ingraham—his hands shake when he isn't using them, and when he is, he has other tics and twitches."

"That doesn't have to mean drugs," Blake said. "What about the woman?"

"Well . . . no twitches, but if you think I'm too outspoken, wait until you meet her."

"What did she say?"

Uncharacteristically, Rane looked away. "It wasn't anything that would help. I don't want to repeat it."

Keira touched Rane's arm to get her attention. "Was it about you being more likely to survive than the two of us? Because if it was, we got that too."

"Yes."

"Plus?"

"Kerry, I'm not going to tell you."

It must have been bad then. There was very little Rane would hesitate to say. Blake resolved to get it out of her later. Now, Eli was coming toward them, motioning them into the wood-and-stone house. The dark-haired woman, Meda, came with him, stopping abruptly in front of Blake so that he had to stop or collide with her. She was a tall bony woman with no attractiveness at all beyond the long, thick, dark brown hair. She may have been attractive once, but now she had no shape, poor coloring, and not even the sense to cover herself as Keira had. She wore jeans cut off at mid-thigh and a man's short-sleeved shirt, buttoned to her skinny midriff, then tied. Blake wondered whether Rane might be right about the drugs.

"For your own sake," Meda said quietly, "you ought to know that we can hear better than most people. I don't usually care who hears what I say, but you might. Now what I told your kid, what she was too embarrassed to repeat, was that I meant to ask Eli for you. I like your looks. It doesn't matter whether you like mine. Everybody here looks like me, sooner or later."

"Jesus Christ," Blake muttered disgustedly. He began to laugh, not meaning to, but not able to stop. "You *are* crazy," he said, still laughing. "All of you." The laughter died finally, and he could only stare at them. They stared back impassively.

"What are you going to do?" he asked Eli. "Give me to her?"

"How can I?" Eli asked. "I don't think I own you. Meda and your kid have a way with words, Doc. With more people like them, we never would have avoided World War Three."

Blake managed to stifle more laughter. He rubbed a hand across his forehead, and was surprised to find it wet. He was standing in the hot desert sun, but between his daughters and his captors, he had hardly noticed.

"What are you going to do with me?" he asked.

"Oh, you'll spend some time with her. That can't be helped. I wish it weren't necessary, but she's your jailer—which is what she was really asking to be. We're going to have to confine you pretty closely for a while, and things will work out better if your jailer is a woman."

"Why?"

"You'll know, Doc. Just give it a little more time. Meanwhile, for the record, what you and Meda do together is your business." He turned, faced Meda. "There are limits," he said softly. "You're getting to like this too goddamn much, you know?"

She glared at him for a moment. "You should talk," she said harshly, though somehow, not quite angrily. She turned and went inside, slamming the door behind her.

Eli sighed. "Lord, I hope you'll all make it—all three of you so we won't have to do this again soon." He glanced to where Ingraham stood watching, managed a crooked smile. "You figure she'll feed us?"

"She'll feed me," Ingraham said, smiling. "She invited me to dinner. Let's go in and see if she's set a place for you."

They herded Blake and the girls into the house, somehow

communicating amusement, weariness, hunger, but no threat. It was almost as though the Maslin family had been invited to eat with new friends. Blake shook his head. On his own, he would have tried to break away from these people—whatever they were —long ago. Now . . . He wondered what his chances were of getting Eli alone, getting his gun and the car keys. If he didn't move soon, Rane or Keira might be separated from him again. These people were in such bad physical condition, they had to take precautions.

Abruptly, it occurred to him that a simple precaution might be to drug something they were to eat or drink.

"What are you planning, Doc?" Eli asked as he sat down in a big, leather wing chair.

The house was cool and dark, comfortably well-kept and old. Blake had to fight off the feeling of security it seemed to offer. He sat on a sofa with his daughters on either side of him.

"Doc?" Eli said.

Blake looked at him.

"I wonder if I can stop you from getting hurt."

"Forget it," Ingraham said. "He's going to have to try something. Just like you'd have to in his place."

"Yeah. Listen, you still have that knife?"

"Sure."

Eli nodded, gestured with one hand. "Come on."

"You mark the wall and Meda'll find some way to get you, man."

"I'm not going to mark the damn wall. Come on."

"Don't break my knife either." Ingraham reached toward his boot, then his hand seemed to blur. Something flashed toward Eli, Eli blurred, and the floorboards beneath Blake's feet vibrated. Blake looked down, saw that there was a large, heavy knife buried in the floor between his feet. It had hit the wood just short of the oriental rug. He gave Eli a single outraged glance, then seized the knife, meaning to pull it free. It remained rooted where it was. He pulled again, using all his strength. Still the knife did not move. It occurred to him that he was making a fool of himself. He sat up straight and glared at Eli.

Eli looked tired and unamused. "Just a trick, Doc." He got up, walked over, and tugged the knife free with little apparent effort. With one long arm, he handed it handle-first to Ingraham, while keeping his attention on Blake. "I know we look scrawny and sick," he said. "We look like one of us alone would equal nothing at all. But if you're going to survive, you have to understand that guns or no guns, you're no match for us. We're faster, better coordinated, stronger, and some other things you wouldn't believe yet."

"You think a circus trick is going to make us believe you're superhuman?" Rane demanded. Blake had felt her jump and cringe when the knife hit. She had been frightened, so now she had to attack. His first impulse was to shut her up, but he held back, remembering the value Eli had placed on her. Eli might tell her to shut up himself, but he would not hurt her just for talking. And she might get something out of him.

"We're not superhuman," Eli said quietly. "We're not anything you won't be eventually. We're just . . . different."

"And sometimes you hurt," Keira whispered.

Eli looked at her—looked until she stopped studying the pattern on the rug and looked back. "It isn't like your pain," he said. "It isn't as clean as your pain."

"Clean?"

"Mine is kind of like what an addict might feel when he tries to kick his habit."

"Drugs?"

"No drugs, I promise you. We don't even use aspirin here."

"I use things. I have to."

"We won't stop you."

"What are you?" she pleaded suddenly. "Please tell us."

Eli put his hands behind his back, though not before Blake noticed that they were trembling.

"Hey," Ingraham said softly. "You okay?"

Eli glanced at him angrily. "No, I'm not okay. Are you okay?"

Keira looked from one of them to the other, then spoke to Eli. "What is it you're keeping yourself from doing to me?"

"Kerry," Rane cautioned. That was a switch—Rane cautioning. Blake wanted to stop Keira himself, would have stopped her, had he not wanted an answer as badly as she did.

"Give me your hands," Eli said to her.

"No!" Blake said, suddenly wary.

But Keira was already extending her hands, palms up, toward Eli. Blake grabbed her hands and pulled them down.

"You made a promise!" he said to Eli. "You said you'd keep her safe!"

"Yes." Eli's coloring looked worse than ever in the cool dimness of the room. His voice was almost too soft to be heard. "I said that." He was perspiring heavily.

"What were you going to do?"

"Answer her question. Nothing else."

Blake did not believe him, but saw no point in saying so. Eli smiled as though Blake had spoken the thought aloud anyway. He unclasped his hands, and Blake noticed that even they were dripping wet. Diaphoresis, Blake thought. Excessive sweating—symptomatic of what? Emaciation, trembling, bad coloring, now sweating—plus surprising strength, speed, and coordination. God knew what else. *Symptomatic of what?*

"Want to hear something funny, Doc?" Eli said in an oddly distant voice. He held his wrist where Blake could see it and pointed to a small double scar that looked black against his gray-brown skin. "A couple of weeks ago while I was helping with the building, I got careless about where I put my hand. A rattlesnake bit me." Eli laughed hollowly. "You know, the damn thing died."

He turned stiffly and went to the door, no longer laughing.

"Eli?" Ingraham said.

"I got to get out of here for a while, man, I'm getting punchy. I'll be back." Eli stumbled out the door and away from the house. When Blake could no longer hear him, he spoke to Ingraham. "That did look like a snakebite scar," he said.

"What the hell do you think it was?" demanded Ingraham. "I was there. The rattler bit him, tried to crawl off, then doubled up a few times and died. We kept the tail. Fifteen-bead rattle."

Blake decided he was being lied to. He sighed and leaned back in silent rejection of whatever fantasy might come next.

Then there was a thunderous sound—a shot, he realized. The dog landed awkwardly, unhurt, but startled by the sound. There was human shouting. Someone pulled the dog back before it could renew its attack.

He looked up and saw a man standing over him, holding an old shotgun. In that brief moment, he noted that the man was frightened both of him and for him, that the man did not want to do harm, but certainly would in self-defense, that this man, according to his body language, would not harm anything helpless.

That was enough.

He let his weariness, hunger, and pain take him. Leaving his abused body to the care of the stranger with the out-of-date conscience and the old-fashioned shotgun, he passed out.

When he came to, he was in a big, cool, blue-walled room, lying in a clean, comfortable bed. He smiled, lay still for a while, taking mental inventory of his already nearly healed injuries. His arm had been bitten and torn in three places. His hands and arms had been scratched and bruised. His legs were bruised. Some of this was from climbing the rocks to this house. Some was from climbing out of the red volcanic mountains where he had hidden when the ship was destroyed. His muscles ached and he was thirsty again. But more important, he was intensely hungry. Food was available now. He could smell it. Someone was cooking pork, roasting it, he thought, so that the savory meat smell drifted through the house and seemed almost edible itself. His body required more food than a normal person's and in spite of his desert kills, he had been hungry for days. The food smells now made him almost sick with hunger.

He found a pitcher of water and a glass on the night table next to his bed. He drank all the water directly from the pitcher, then sat up and looked himself over.

He had been bathed, and clothed in someone's gray pajamas. Whoever had removed his coverall and bathed him was probably ill. They would not realize it for about three weeks, but when the symptoms began to make themselves felt, chances were, his res-

"This whole thing is going to be hard on you, L
graham said. "You're going to want to ignore just abou
thing we say because none of it makes any sense in the wo
come from. You'll deny and Rane will try to deny and it
make a damn bit of difference because one way or anothe
three of you are here to stay."

PAST 5

The dogs were winning.

They had attacked almost in unison, furiously, angered by
his alien scent. Together, they managed to bring him down before
he could hurt either of them. Then the smaller one, who appeared
to be part Doberman, bit into the arm he had thrown up to
protect his throat.

Pain was the trigger that threw him into his changed body's
version of overdrive. Moving faster than the dogs could follow, he
rolled, came to his feet, locked both hands together and battered
the smaller dog down in midair. The dog gave a short shrieking
cry, fell, and lay twitching on the ground.

The larger dog leaped for his throat. He threw himself to one
side, avoiding its teeth, but hunger and weariness had taken their
toll. He stumbled, fell. The dog lunged again. He knew he could
not avoid it this time, knew he was about to die.

cuer would go to a doctor and pass the infection on beyond this isolated place. And chances were, neither the rescuer nor the doctor would survive—though, of course, both would live long enough to infect others. Many others. Both would be infectious long before they began to exhibit symptoms. The doctor would not recognize the illness, would probably give it first to family and friends.

The ship had died, the three people he had come to love most had died with it to prevent the epidemic he had probably just begun. He should have died with them. But of the four, only his enhanced survival drive had saved him—much against his will. He had been a prisoner within his own skull, cut off from conscious control of his body. He had watched himself running for cover, saving himself, and thus nullifying the sacrifice of the others. To his sorrow, to his ultimate shame, he, and he alone, had brought the first extraterrestrial life to Earth.

What could he do now? Could he do anything? Was not the whole matter literally out of his hands? Had it ever been otherwise?

A woman came into the room. She was tall and rangy and about fifty—too old to attract his interest in any dangerous way.

"So," she said, "you're among the living again. I thought you might be. Are you hungry?"

"Yes," he croaked. He coughed and tried again. "Please, yes."

"Coming right up," the woman said. "By the way, what's your name?"

"Jake," he lied. "Jacob Moore." Jake Moore had been his maternal grandfather, a good man, an old-style, shouting Baptist preacher who had stepped in and taken the place of his father when his father died. It was a name he would not forget, no matter how his body distracted him. His own name would send this woman hurrying to the nearest phone or radio or whatever people in this desolate place used to communicate with the world outside. She would call the would-be rescuers he had hidden from for three days after the destruction of the ship, and she would feel that she had done him a great favor. Then how many people would he be driven to infect before someone realized what was happening?

Or was he wrong? Should he give himself up? Would he be able to tell everything he knew and dump the problem and himself into the laps of others?

The moment the thought came to him, he knew it was impossible. To give himself up would be an act of self-destruction. He would be confined, isolated. He would be prevented from doing the one thing he *must* do: seeking out new hosts for the alien microorganisms that had made themselves such fundamental parts of his body. Their purpose was now his purpose, and their only purpose was to survive and multiply. All his increased strength, speed, coordination, and sensory ability was to keep him alive and mobile, able to find new hosts or beget them. Many hosts. Perhaps three out of four of those found would die, but that magical fourth was worth any amount of trouble.

The organisms were not intelligent. They could not tell him how to keep himself alive, free, and able to find new hosts. But they became intensely uncomfortable if he did not, and their discomfort was his discomfort. He might interpret what they made him feel as pleasure when he did what was necessary, desirable, *essential;* or as pain when he tried to do what was terrifying, self-destructive, *impossible.* But what he was actually feeling were secondhand advance-retreat responses of millions of tiny symbionts.

The woman touched him to get his attention. She had brought him a tray. He took it on his lap, trying, and in the final, driven instant, failing to return the woman's kindness. He could not spare her. He scratched her wrist just hard enough to draw blood.

"I'm sorry," he said at once. "The rocks . . ." He displayed his jagged nails. "Sorry."

"It's nothing," the woman said. "I'd like to hear how you wound up out here so far from any other settlement. And here." She handed him a linen napkin—real linen. "Wipe your hands and face. Why are you perspiring so? It's cool in here."

PRESENT 6

In surprisingly little time, Meda served a huge meal. There was a whole ham—Blake wondered whether it was homegrown —several chickens, more salad than Blake thought six people could possibly eat, corn on the cob, buttered carrots, green beans, baked potatoes, rolls . . . Blake suspected this was the first meal he had eaten that contained almost nothing from boxes, bags, or cans. Not even salt on most of the food, he realized unhappily. He wondered whether the food was clean and free of live parasites. Could some parasite, some worm, perhaps, be responsible for these people's weight loss? Parasitic worm infestations were almost unknown now, but these people had not chosen to live in the present. They had adopted a nineteenth-century lifestyle. Perhaps they had contracted a nineteenth-century disease. Yet they were strong and alert. If they were sharing their bodies with worms, the worms were damned unusual.

Blake picked at the barely seasoned food, eating little of it. He wasn't concerned about any possible worm infestation. That could be taken care of easily once he was free. And since everyone took food from the same serving dishes, selective drugging was impossible. He let the girls eat their fill. And he watched the abductors—especially Eli—eat prodigious amounts.

Keira tried to talk to him during the meal, but he gave the impression of being too busy eating to listen. Blake thought he tried a little too hard to give that impression. Eli was attracted to Keira; that was obvious. Blake hoped his ignoring her meant he was rejecting the attraction. The girl was sixteen, naïve, and sheltered. Like most enclave parents, Blake had done all he could to recreate the safe world of perhaps sixty years past for his children. Enclaves were islands surrounded by vast, crowded, vulnerable residential areas through which ran sewers of utter lawlessness connecting cesspools—economic ghettos that regularly chewed their inhabitants up and spat the pieces into surrounding communities. The girls knew about such things only superficially. Neither of them would know how to handle a grown man who saw them as fair game. Nothing had ever truly threatened them before.

Meda was staring at Blake.

She must have been doing it for some time now. She had eaten her meal—a whole, roasted chicken plus generous helpings of everything else. Now she nibbled at a thick slice of ham and stared.

"What is it?" he asked her.

She looked at Eli. "Why wait?" she asked.

"God knows I almost didn't," he said. "Do what you want to."

She got up, walked around the table, stood over Blake, staring down at him intently. Sweat ran down her thin, predatory face. "Come on, Doc," she whispered.

Blake was afraid of her. It was ridiculous, but he was afraid.

"Get up," she said. "Come on. Believe it or not, I don't like to humiliate people."

Sweat ran into her eyes, but she did not seem to notice. In a moment, she would take hold of him with her skinny claws. He stood up, stiff with fear of the woman and fear of showing it. He bumped the table, palmed a knife, secretly, he thought. The idea of threatening her with it, maybe using it on her, repelled him, but he gripped it tightly.

"Bring the knife if you want to," she said. "I don't care."

She turned and walked to the hall door. There she stood, waiting.

"Dad," Keira said anxiously. "Please . . . do what they say."

He looked at her, saw that she was frightened too.

She looked from him to Eli, but Eli would not meet her eyes. She faced Blake again. "Dad, don't make them hurt you."

What was it about these people? How were they able to terrify when they did nothing? It was as though there were something other than human about them. Or was it only their several guns?

"Dad," Rane said, "do it. They're crazy."

He looked at Eli. If the girls were hurt in any way—any way at all—Eli would pay. Eli seemed to be in charge. He could permit harm or prevent it. If he did not prevent it, no circus trick would save him.

Eli stared back, and Blake felt that he understood. Eli had shown himself to be unusually perceptive. And now he looked almost as miserable as Blake felt.

Blake turned and followed Meda. He kept the knife. Everyone saw it now, and they let him keep it. That alone was almost enough to make him leave it. They managed to make him feel like a fool for wanting a weapon against armed people who had kidnapped him and his children at gunpoint. But he would have felt like a bigger fool if he had left the knife behind.

Meda led him into a back bedroom with blue walls, a solid, heavy door, and barred windows.

"My daughter is going to need her medication," he said, wondering why he had not spoken of it to Eli.

"Eli will take care of her," the woman said. Blake thought he heard bitterness in her voice, but her face was expressionless.

"He doesn't know what she needs."

"She knows, doesn't she?" In the instant before he could lie, Meda nodded. "I thought she did. Give me the knife, Blake." She said it quietly as she locked the door and turned to face him. She saw his refusal before he could voice it. "I didn't want to tear into you in front of your kids," she said. "Human nature being what it is, you probably wouldn't be able to forgive me for that as quickly as you'll forgive me for . . . other things. But in here, I'm not going to hold back. I don't have the patience."

"What are you talking about?"

She reached out so quickly that by the time he realized she had moved, she had him by the wrist in a grip just short of bone-cracking. As she forced the knife from his captive hand, he hit at her. He had never hit a woman with his fist before, but he had had enough from this one.

His fist met only air. Inhumanly fast, inhumanly strong, the woman dodged his blow. She caught his fist in her crushing grip.

He lurched against her to throw her off-balance. She fell, dragging him with her, cursing him as they hit the floor. The knife was still between them in one of his captive hands. He fought desperately to keep it, believing that at any moment the noise would draw one or both of the men into the room. What would they do to him for attacking her? He was committed. He had to keep the knife and, if necessary, threaten to use it on her. His daughters were not the only people who could be held as hostages.

The woman tried to get him off her. He had managed to fall on top and he weighed perhaps twice what she did. As strong as she was, she did not seem to know how to fight. She managed to take the knife and throw it off to one side so that it skittered under a chair. Angrily, he tried to punch her again. This time he connected. She went limp.

She was not unconscious; only stunned. She tried feebly to stop him when he went after the knife, but she no longer had the strength.

The knife was embedded in the wall behind the chair. Before he could pull it free, she was on him again. This time, she hit him. While he lay semiconscious, she retrieved the knife, opened a window, and threw it out between the bars. Then she staggered back to him, sat down on the floor next to him, hugging her knees, resting her forehead against them. She did not look as though she could see him. She was temptingly close, and as his vision cleared, he was tempted.

"You start that shit again, I'll break your jaw!" she muttered. She stretched out on the rug beside him, rubbing her jaw. "If I break your bones, you won't survive," she said. "You'll be like those damn bikers. We had to hurt them because there were too many of them for us to take it easy. All but two wound up with broken bones or other serious injuries. They died."

"They died of their injuries . . . or of a disease?"

"It's a disease," she said.

"Have I been infected?"

She turned her head to look at him, smiled sadly. "Oh yes."

"The food?"

"No. The food was just food. Me."

"Contact?"

"No, inoculation." She lifted his right arm, exposing the bloody scratches she had made. They hurt now that she had drawn his attention to them.

"You would have done that even if I hadn't had the knife?" he asked.

"Yes."

"All right, you've done it. Get away from me."

"No, we'll talk now. You're our first doctor. We've wanted one for a long time."

Blake said nothing.

"It's something like a virus," she said. "Except that it can live and multiply on its own for a few hours if it has warmth and moisture."

Then it wasn't a virus, he thought. She didn't know what she was talking about.

"It likes to attach itself to cells the way a virus does," she continued. "It can multiply that way too. Don't tune me out yet, Blake," she said. "I'm no doctor, but I have information for you. Maybe you can use it to help yourself and your kids."

That got his attention. He sat up, climbed painfully into the antique wooden rocking chair that he had shoved aside when he tried to reach the knife. "I'll listen," he said.

"It's a virus-sized microbe," she said. "Filtrable. I hear that means damned small."

"Who told you?"

She looked surprised. "Eli. Who else?"

He could not quite bring himself to ask whether Eli was a doctor.

"He was a minister for a while," she said as though he had asked. "A boy minister at the turn of the century when the country was full of ministers. Then he went to college and became a geologist. He married a doctor."

Blake frowned at her. "What are you going to tell me now? That you're telepathic?"

She shook her head. "I wish we were. We read body language. We see things you wouldn't even notice—things we didn't notice before. We don't work at it; it isn't a conscious thing. Among ourselves, it's communication. With strangers, it's protection."

"Why haven't you gotten treatment?"

"What treatment?"

"You haven't tried to get any treatment, have you? What about Eli's wife? Hasn't she—"

"She's dead. The disease killed her."

Blake stared at her. "Good God. And you've deliberately given it to me?"

"Yes," she said. "I know it doesn't make sense to you. It wouldn't have to me before. But now . . . You'll understand eventually. And when you do, I hope you'll accept our way of living. It's so damn hard when people don't. Like having one of my kids go wrong."

Blake tried to make sense of this. Before he could give up on her again, she got up and went over to him.

"It isn't necessary for you to understand now," she said. "For now, just listen and ask questions if you want to. Pretend you believe me." She touched his face. Repelled, he caught her hand and pushed it away. His cheek hurt a little and he realized she had scratched him again. He touched his face and his hand came away bloody.

"What the hell are you going to do?" he demanded. "Keep scratching me as long as you can find a few inches of clear skin?"

"Not that bad," she said softly. "I don't understand why— maybe you will—but people with original infections at the neck or above get the disease faster. And infected people who get a lot of attention from us usually survive. The organism doesn't use cells up the way a virus does. It combines with them, lives with them, divides with them, changes them just a little. Eli says it's a symbiont, not a parasite."

"But it kills," Blake said.

"Sometimes." She sounded defensive. "Sometimes people work hard to die. Those bikers, for instance . . . . I took care of Orel—Ingraham, I mean. His first name's Orel. He hates it. Anyway, I took care of him. He didn't like me much then, but he let me. He survived okay. But the other biker who had a chance was a real bastard. Lupe stuck with him, but he kept trying to kill her—strangling, smothering, beating . . . When he tried to burn her to death in her sleep, she got mad and hit him too hard. Broke his neck."

Blake put most of this aside for later consideration and focused on one implication. "Are you planning to sleep here?" he demanded.

She smiled. "Get used to the idea. After all, I can't very well rape you, can I?"

He did not answer. He was thinking about his daughters.

She drew a deep breath, touched his hand without scratching this time. "I'm sorry," she said. "I'm told I have the sensitivity of a hunk of granite sometimes. None of us are rapists here. No one is going to take your kids to bed against their wills."

"So you say!"

"It's true. Our men don't rape. They don't have to."

"You haven't had to do any of the things you've done."

"But we have. Like I said, you'll understand eventually. For now, you'll just have to accept what I tell you. We're changed, but we have ethics. We aren't animals."

Blake thought that was exactly what they were, but he kept quiet. There was no point in arguing with her. But Rane and Keira . . . What was happening to them?

Meda took a chair from the desk on the other side of the room and brought it over so that she could sit next to him. He watched her swing her thin body around. She moved like a man.

She must have been a powerful-looking woman before her illness. Yet the illness had reduced her to wiry thinness. What would it do to Keira who had no weight to lose, who already had a disease that was slowly killing her?

Meda sat down and took his hands. "I wish you could believe me," she said. "This is the worst time for you. I wish I could help more."

"Help!" He snatched his hands away from her, disgusted. She was still perspiring heavily. In a cool room, she was soaking wet. And no doubt the perspiration was loaded with disease organisms. "You've 'helped' enough!"

She wiped her face and smiled grimly. "You still bring out the worst in me. You don't feel or smell like one of us—like an infected person—yet."

"Smell?"

"Oh yes. Part of your body language, part of your identity is your odor. And one of your earliest symptoms is going to be suddenly smelling things you never consciously noticed before. Eli found our place by following his nose. He was lost in the desert. We had water, and he smelled it."

"He came here? This was your home, then?"

". . . yes."

He wondered about her sudden pensiveness, but took no time to question it. He had something more important to ask. "Where did Eli come from, Meda? Where did he catch the disease?"

She hesitated. "Look, I'll tell you if you want me to. It's my job to explain things to you. But there are some things you'll have to understand before I tell you about Eli. First, like I said, I scratched your face just now so you'd get sick sooner. Most people take about three weeks to start feeling symptoms. Sometimes a little longer. You'll feel yours a lot sooner—and you should be infectious in a few days."

"That could mean I'll die sooner," Blake said.

"I'm not going to give you up that easily," she said. "You're going to make it!"

"Why did you rush things for me?"

"We're afraid of you. We want you on our side because you might be able to help us save more converts—that's what Eli calls them. We . . . we care about the people we lose. But we have to be sure of you, and we can't until you're one of us. Right now, you're sort of in-between. You're not one of us yet, but you're . . . not normal either. If you escaped now and managed to reach other people, you'd eventually give them the disease. You'd spread it to everyone you could reach, and you wouldn't be able to stay and help them. Nobody can fight the compulsion alone. We need each other."

"Who did Eli have?" Blake asked. "His wife?"

"He had nobody. That was the problem. But before I get into that, I want to be sure you understand that there's no way to leave here without starting an epidemic. The compulsion quiets down a little after you've been sick. You should have enough control then to go into town and buy whatever you'll need that isn't in that computerized bag Eli says you have."

"Buy medical supplies?"

"Yes."

"You're going to trust me enough to let me go into town?"

"Yes, but nobody travels alone. There's too much temptation to do harm. Blake, you aren't ever going to be comfortable among ordinary people again."

He didn't know how he would have felt if he had believed her. But in fact, he meant to take any opportunity to escape that came his way. He did not intend to live his life as an emaciated carrier of a deadly disease. Yet he was afraid. Some of what Meda had said about the disease reminded him of another illness—one he had read about years before. He could not remember the name of it. It was something people did not get any longer—something old and deadly that people had once gotten from animals. And the animals had gone out of their way to spread it. The name came to him suddenly: rabies.

She watched him silently. "You don't believe me, but you're afraid," she said. "That's a start. There's a lot to be afraid of."

He stifled an impulse to deny his fear or explain it. "You were going to tell me about Eli," he said.

She nodded. "Remember that ship a few years ago—the *Clay's Ark?*"

"The *Ark?* You mean the starship?"

"Yeah. Brand new technology, tested all to hell, and it still blew up when it got back from the Centauri system. People figured the scientists rushed things so they would have something flashy to keep them from losing their funding again. At least, that's what I read. The *Ark* came down about thirty miles from here. It was supposed to land at one of the space stations or on the moon, but it came all the way home. And before it blew up, Eli got out."

"Eli . . . ? What are you telling me?"

"His name is Asa Elias Doyle. He was their geologist. In case you haven't noticed, he can drop that dumb accent of his whenever he wants to. The disease is from the second planet of Proxima Centauri. It killed ten of a crew of fourteen. I think more would have lived, but they began by isolating anyone who got sick. Then they found they had to restrain them to keep them isolated." She shuddered. "That amounted to slow death by torture.

"Anyway, four survived to come home. I think they had to come home. The compulsion drove them. But when they landed something went wrong. Maybe for once, someone managed to break the compulsion. The ship was destroyed. Only Eli managed to get out. But in one way, that didn't matter. He brought Proxi Two back to us as well as a crew of fourteen could have. And now . . . now it's as Terran as you or me."

PAST 7

A few minutes of careful listening told him there were seven people sharing the isolated wood-and-stone house with him. There were the two adult sons and a twenty-year-old daughter, who had spent the night in Barstow. There was their mother, who had brought food and who had been kind, and the sons' new young wives, who were eager for the separate houses to be finished. There was the white-haired patriarch of the household —a stern man who believed in an outdated, angry God and who knew how to use a shotgun. He reminded himself of this last when he met the daughter. Meda, her name was.

Meda introduced herself by walking into the room he had been given just as he pulled on a borrowed pair of pants. And instead of retreating when she saw that he was dressing, she stayed to watch. He was so glad she was not the woman of the night before, the woman whose scent had frozen him outside her window, that her brazenness did not bother him. This one's scent was far more interesting than a man's would have been, but she had not yet reached that dangerous time in her cycle. She was big like her mother—perhaps six feet tall, and stocky where her mother was becoming old-woman thin. Meda was brown-haired, heavily tanned, and strong-looking—probably used to hard work.

She stared at him curiously and was unable to conceal her disappointment at his thin, wiry body. He did not blame her. He was disgusted with his appearance himself, though he knew how deceptive it was. He had been good-looking once. Women had never been a problem for him.

This woman, however, was a problem already. Her expression said she recognized him. That was completely unexpected— that someone in this isolated place would keep up with current events enough to know what one of fourteen astronauts looked like. Unfortunately, his face had changed less than the rest of him. It had always been thin. And with the *Ark* returning, there must have been a great rebroadcasting and republishing of old pictures. This woman had probably just seen several of them in Barstow.

"How have you lost so much weight?" she asked as he pulled on a shirt. The clothing belonged to Gabriel Boyd, the father of the family. He was thin, too, though not quite as tall. The pants were too short. "You look like you haven't eaten for weeks," Meda said.

"I am hungry," he admitted.

"My mother says you just ate enough for two people."

He shrugged. He was still hungry. He was going to have to do something about it soon.

"We don't have a videophone," she said, "or a telephone, or even a radio."

"That's okay. I don't want to call anyone."

"Why not?"

He did not answer.

"What do you want?" she asked.

"I want you to get out of here before your father or one of your brothers gets the wrong idea."

"This is my room."

That did not surprise him. The room did not look as though it belonged to a young woman. There was no clothing in sight, no perfume or makeup, no frills. But it smelled of her. The bed smelled of her.

"I was in Barstow with my brothers overnight," she said. "There are some supplies my brothers can't be trusted to buy, even with a list." She gave him a sad smile. "So I went to the big city."

"Barstow?" Like most desert towns, it had been water-short and shrinking for years—not that it had ever been big.

"Anything bigger would be too sinful. It might tempt me or contaminate me or something. You know, I've only been to L.A. twice in my life."

He wiped his wet face with dripping hands. She did not know how she tempted him to contaminate her. His compulsion was to touch her, take her hands perhaps, scratch or bite if she pulled away. Sex would have been very satisfying with her, too, though not as satisfying as when she reached her fertile time. She was not the kind of woman who would have attracted him in any way at all before. Now all a woman had to do to attract him was smell uncontaminated.

He looked away from her, sweat soaking into his borrowed clothing. "You're not missing anything by keeping away from cities," he said. He had been born in a so-called middle-class residential area of that same vast, deadly Los Angeles she wanted more of, and if not for his grandfather, he would probably already have died there. Many of the people he had grown up with had died of too much L.A. A girl like this one, not pretty, eager for attention and excitement, would not survive a year in L.A.

"We barely have running water here," she grumbled.

Fool. She had clean, sweet well water here, free for the taking. In stinking L.A., she would have a limited amount of flat, desalinized, purified, expensive ocean water. In L.A., you could tell how little money a man had by how bad he smelled. "You don't know when you're well off," he told her. "But if you're crazy enough to want to try city life, why don't you just move?"

She shrugged, looking surprisingly young and vulnerable. "I'm afraid," she admitted. "I guess I haven't cut the umbilical yet. But I'm working on it." She fell silent for a moment, then said, "Asa?"

He looked at her sidelong. "Girl, even my enemies have more sense than to call me that."

"Elias then," she said, smiling.

"Eli."

"Okay."

"You tell anybody?"

"No."

That was true. She was enjoying having the secret too much to give it away. Now he had to keep her quiet.

"Why are you here?" she asked. "Why aren't you being debriefed or paraded down some big city street or something?"

Why was he not in isolation, she meant. Why was he not waiting and contending with a misery no one but him could understand while a dozen doctors discovered what a dangerous man he was? Why was he not dead in an escape attempt? And considering the loss of the ship, its wealth of data, its frozen, dead crew, and its diseased, living crew, debriefing was a laughably mild name for what he would have been put through.

"What's the matter?" Meda asked softly. She had a big voice, not intended for speaking softly, but she managed. She had come closer. God help her, why didn't she go away? Why didn't he order her away or leave himself?

She touched his arm. "Are you all right?"

His body went on automatic. Helplessly, he grasped her hand. He managed not to scratch her, and tried to feel good about that until he saw that she had a small abrasion on the back of her hand. That was enough. His touch would probably have been enough anyway. Eventually she would have eaten something with that hand or scratched her lip or wiped her mouth or scratched or licked her hand to quiet the slight itching sensation contamination sometimes produced. And the disease organism could live on the skin for hours in spite of normal, haphazard hand-washing. Any person he touched was almost certainly doomed in one way or another.

"Why are your hands wet?" she asked. And when he did not answer, she examined his hands. He had expected her to drop them in disgust, but she did not seem disgusted. She was a big,

strong girl. Maybe she could be saved. Maybe he could save her
—if he stayed.

He remembered trying vainly to save his wife, Disa. She had
been a short, slender woman with no weight to lose, barely big
enough to qualify for the space program. The disease had eaten
her alive. She had been one of the mission's two M.D.s, however,
and before she died, she and Grove Kenyon, the other doctor, had
discovered that the disease organism caused changes that could
be beneficial—if the host survived its initial onslaught. Surviving
hosts became utterly resistant to more conventional diseases and
more efficient at performing certain specialized functions. Only
the toxin excreted by the disease organism was life-threatening.
Not surprisingly, the human body had no defense against it. But
in time the organism changed, adapted, and chemically encour-
aged its host to adapt. Its by-products ceased to be toxic to its host
and the host ceased to react as strongly to increased sexual needs
and heightened sensory awareness—inevitable effects of the disease. The needed time was bought by new organisms of the same
disease—new organisms introduced after significant adaptation
had occurred. The new, unadapted organisms quickly spent themselves neutralizing the toxic wastes of the old. Thus, the new
organisms had to be replaced frequently. The host body was a
hostile environment for them—an environment already occupied,
claimed, chemically marked by others of their kind. Their toxin-
neutralization was merely their reflexive effort to survive in that
hostile environment.

But the original invading organisms had too much of a start.
Or, if they were not well started, if the new organisms were
introduced too soon, those new organisms simply became part of
the original invasion, and the host, the patient, was no better, no
worse.

The meager statistics provided by the crew and the few
experimental animals they managed to raise from frozen embryos
seemed to support these findings. All four of the surviving crew
members had been reinfected several times. There were no survi-
vors among the first crew members stricken. These had been
isolated and restrained. Their vital functions had been continually

monitored and restored when they failed. But finally their brains had ceased to function.

Reinfection was the answer, then—or *an* answer. A partial answer. Without it, everyone died. With it, some lived. Disa had died. Meda was obviously stronger. Perhaps she could live.

PRESENT 8

Meda brought Blake his bag when he asked for it and permitted him to examine her. She even permitted him to cleanse the scratches she had made on his arm and face, though she warned it would do no good. It had never done any good before when someone was infected, she said. The organisms were aggressive and fast. He had the disease.

She or someone else had found and sabotaged his panic button with one of the newer permanent glues. With these, permanent meant permanent. He could not use the bag to call for help. Otherwise, the bag was intact. For Keira's sake in particular, it was one of the best. His scope would probably give him a look at the *Clay's Ark* organism, even if it was as small as Meda had said. He needed all the information he could get before he made his escape. It was not only a matter of his wanting to pass the information on. He also needed to know now of any weaknesses these people had. They were too good to be true in every way except appearance. He had to find something he could use against them.

"I could have used you when my children were born," Meda told him as he took her blood pressure.

"Didn't you have a doctor?" he asked. He checked her pulse.

"No. Just Eli and Lorene, my sister-in-law. We don't bring anyone here if we don't plan to keep them. And I didn't dare go to a hospital. Imagine how many people I'd infect there."

"Not if you told them the truth."

She watched as he drew blood from her left arm. It went directly into the analyzer as would all her other specimens. "They'd put me in a goddamn cage," she said. "They'd put my kids in one, too. They were born with the disease, you know."

"Did they have any special problems?"

She turned her head to stare directly at him. "Not a one," she said. She made no effort to conceal the fact that she was lying.

"What about you?" Blake asked gently. "Easy births?"

"Yeah," she said. Her defensiveness vanished. "The first one really surprised me. I mean, I was scared. I expected to be in agony, and I don't handle real pain that well. But the kid popped out with no trouble at all. Felt like cramps."

"You were lucky there was no emergency. May I see your children?"

"Not until you're safe, Blake."

"Safe?"

"When you've been sick and gotten well again, then we'll have nothing to worry about. We'll show you anything you want."

He frowned. "Do you imagine I'd hurt a child?"

"Probably not," she said. "But you're at the seeking-weakness stage, and Jacob and Joseph would be a hell of a weakness. If you used them, we'd have to kill you. We want you alive, Blake."

He looked away from her in growing desperation. They really were too good—always a step ahead. How many times had they done this—abducted people, made them vanish from the world outside. He had to beat them at a game they knew all too well. But how?

Meda rubbed his arm with a wet hand. "Look," she said, "it

isn't so bad here. You can do a lot of good—maybe more good than you could do anywhere else. You can help us prevent an epidemic."

"It's only a matter of time before your disease gets out of hand," he said.

"We've kept that from happening for more than four years."

"Yet it could happen tomorrow."

"No!" She got up and began to pace. "I can't really make you understand until you've felt it, but we'd go crazy if we were caged. We'd probably kill ourselves trying to escape. The compulsion keeps us on a pretty thin edge as it is. Eli says we're holding on to our humanity by our fingernails. I'm not sure we're holding on to it at all. In some ways, I'm more realistic than he is. But maybe we need a little of his idealism. God knows how he's kept it." She glanced at Blake. "He's my kids' father, you know."

"I guessed," Blake said.

"He helps us hold on even if all we're holding on to is an illusion. Take away that illusion and what's left is something you wouldn't want to deal with. You'll see."

"If your veneer of humanity is that thin," Blake said, "it's only a matter of time before someone finds it too thin. And if what you've told me about the disease is true, one person could infect hundreds and those hundreds could infect thousands—all before the first victims began to show symptoms and realize they were sick."

"Your estimate is low," she said. "Now do you see why you have to stay here? *You* could become that one person."

He did not argue with her. He would escape and go to a hospital; that was all. "I'd like you to undress," he said. He had just collected a little of her sweat and taken—almost painlessly—a minute specimen of her flesh. The analyzer found something incomprehensible in both—probably the same something it had found in her blood and urine.

"Unidentifiable microbes," the small screen said. It was able to show him tiny, spiderlike organisms in her flesh, some of them caught in the act of reproducing along with her cells—*as part of her cells.* They were not viruses. According to the computer, they were more complete, independent organisms. Yet they had made themselves at home in human cells in a way that should not have been possible—like plasmids invading and making themselves at home in bacteria. But these were hardly plasmids—solitary rings of DNA. These were more complex organisms that had sought out higher game than bacteria and managed to combine with it without killing it. They had changed it, however, altered it slightly, subtly, cell by cell. In the most basic possible way, they had tampered with Meda's genetic blueprint. They had left her no longer human.

"The ones that live in the brain don't have little legs—cilia, I mean," Meda said over his shoulder.

"What?"

"Eli told me they get into the brain cells, too. It sounds frightening, but there isn't anything we can do about it. I guess they'd have to reach the brain to change us so."

She did not know how changed she was. Could there be any hope of reversing such elemental changes? There must be, for his daughters' sake.

"Eli and I used to talk about it a lot," she said. "He wanted me to know everything he knew—in case anything happened to him. He said his wife and the other doctor did autopsies on the crew members who died before them. They found little round organisms in the brains of every one of them."

"Rabies again," Blake muttered. But no. Rabies was only a virus, preventable and curable.

"Eli's wife tried to make antibodies," Meda said. "It didn't work. I don't remember what else she tried. I didn't understand, anyway. But nothing worked except reinfection. They found out about that by accident. And it works better person-to-person than person-to-syringe. Maybe that's just psychological, but we don't care. We'll use anything that works. That's why I'm here with you."

"You're here to try to make a good carrier of me," he said.

She shrugged. "You'll be that or die. I'd rather live myself."

There was another answer. There had to be. He could not find it with only his bag, but others, researchers with lab computers, would sooner or later come up with answers. First, though, they had to be made aware of the questions.

He turned to look at Meda and saw that she had stripped. Surprisingly, she looked less scrawny without her clothing. More like the human female she was not. What could her children be like?

She smiled. "All my clothes are too big," she said. "I put them on and I look like a collection of sticks, I know. Maybe now I'll buy a few new things next time I'm in town."

He ignored the obvious implication, but could not ignore the way she kept reading him. He became irrationally afraid that she was reading his mind, that he would never be able to keep an escape plan from her. He tried to shake off the feeling as he proceeded with the examination. She said nothing more. He got the impression she was sparing him, humoring him.

He asked to examine others in the community when he finished with her, but she was not ready to share him with anyone else.

"Start checking them tomorrow if they'll let you," she said. "You'll smell different then. Less seductive."

"Seductive?"

"I mean you'll smell more like one of us. Nobody will take any special pleasure in touching you then." She had dressed again in her loose, ugly clothing. "It's sexual," she said. "Or rather, it feels sexual. Touching you is almost as good as screwing. It would be good even if I didn't like you. If not for people like you— people we have to catch and keep, I could never control myself enough to go into town. With no outlet it gets . . . painful and crazy, sort of frenzied when there are a lot of unconverted people around. I have dreams about suddenly finding myself moving through a crowd—maybe on a big city street. Moving through a crowd where I have no choice but to keep touching people. I don't even know whether to call it a nightmare or not. I'm on automatic. It's just happening."

"You'd like it to happen," he said, watching her.

"Pigshit!" she said, abruptly angry. "If I wanted it to happen, it would happen. I'd get in my car and I'd drive. I could infect people in towns from here to New York. And I'd do exactly that if I ever had to leave this place. There would be no one to help me, stop me." She hesitated, then sat down on the bed beside him. He managed not to recoil when she took his hand. He was getting information from her. Let her touch him as long as she kept talking.

"You've got to understand," she said. "It's really hard on us the way we limit our growth. We can only do it because we're so isolated. But if you escaped—with or without your kids—we'd have to escape too before you could send people here to corral us. I don't know where we'd go, but chances are, we'd have to split up. Now you imagine, for instance, Ingraham out there on his own. He was high-strung before, and damned undisciplined. He doesn't shake because there's more wrong with him than with the rest of us. He shakes because he's holding himself back almost all the time. He respects Eli and he loves Lupe. She's going to have his kid. But you force him out of here, and all by himself, he'll start an epidemic you won't believe."

"And you're saying that will be my fault," Blake said angrily. She was boxing him in. Everything she said was intended to close another exit.

"We'll do *anything* to avoid being locked up," she said. "I'll do *anything* to keep my sons from being taken from me."

"Nobody would take your—"

"Shut your mouth! They'd take them. They'd treat them like things. If they killed them—accidentally or deliberately, it would just be one of their problems solved."

"Meda, listen—"

"So if you're afraid of an epidemic, *Doctor*, don't even think about leaving us. Even if you spread the word, you can't possibly stop us." She switched tracks abruptly. "I'm starving. Do you want anything to eat?"

He was disoriented for a moment. "Food?"

"We eat a lot. You'll see."

"What if you didn't?" he asked, immediately alert. "I mean, I couldn't have put away the meal I saw you eat only a few hours ago. What if you just ate normally?"

"We do eat normally—for us."

"You know what I mean."

"Yeah, I know. You're still seeking weakness. Well, you've found one. We eat a lot. Now what are you going to do? Destroy our food supply?" She produced a key from somewhere, seemingly by magic. Her hands actually were quicker than his eyes. "Don't even think about doing anything to the food," she said. "Someday I'll tell you how people like you smell to my kids." She let herself out and slammed the door behind her.

She returned sometime later, bringing him a ham sandwich and a fruit salad.

"I'd like to see my daughters," he told her.

"I'll see," she said. "Maybe I can bring you one of them for a few minutes."

Her cooperativeness pleased but did not surprise him. She had children of her own and she could see that his concern was genuine; there was no reason for her to find that concern suspect.

He was lying down, tired and frightened, hanging on to the bare bones of an escape plan when Eli brought Keira in.

Keira seemed calm. Eli left her without saying a word. He locked her in and probably stood outside listening.

"Are you all right?" Blake asked.

She answered the question he intended rather than the one he had asked. "He hasn't touched me," she said. She did not sit down, but stood in the middle of the room and looked at Blake. He looked back, realizing that for her sake, he could not touch her either. Such a simple, terrible thing. He could not touch her.

"He said Meda scratched you," she whispered.

Blake nodded.

"He told me about the disease and . . . where he got it. I didn't know what to think. Do you believe him?"

" 'Her' in my case." Blake stared through the bars of the window into the desert night. "I believe. Maybe I shouldn't, but I do."

"Rane always says I'll believe anything. At first, I was afraid to believe this. I do now, though."

"Have you seen Rane?"

"No. Daddy?"

He looked away from the bright full moon, met her eyes and saw that in a moment she would come to him, disease or no disease.

"No!" he said sharply.

"Why?" she demanded. "What difference does it make? Someone's going to touch me sooner or later, anyway. And even if they don't, I've probably already got the disease—from the salad or the bread or the furniture or the dishes . . . What's the difference?" She wiped away tears angrily. She tended to cry when she got upset, whether she wanted to or not.

"Why hasn't he touched you?"

She looked at Blake, looked away. "He likes me. He's afraid he'll kill me."

"I wonder how long that will stop him?"

"Not long. He obviously feels terrible. Sooner or later, he's going to just grab me."

Blake opened his bag again, turned it on, and keyed in a prescription form. "ARE YOU LOCKED UP?" he typed. "ARE YOUR WINDOWS BARRED?"

She shook her head, mouthed, "No bars."

"THEN YOU CAN ESCAPE!"

"Alone?" she mouthed. She shook her head.

"YOU MUST!" he typed. "AT TWO A.M., I'LL TRY. I WANT YOU WITH ME!" Aloud, he said, "I can't help you, Kerry."

"I know," she whispered. "Most of the time, I'm not even worried about myself. I'm worried about you and Rane. I don't even know where Rane is."

He began typing soundlessly again. "THEN BREAK FREE ALONE! THEY THINK YOU'RE HELPLESS. THEY'LL BE CARELESS WITH YOU."

She shook her head as she read the words. "I can't," she mouthed. "I can't!"

"Are you having any pain?" he asked aloud. "Did you take your medicine?"

"No pain," she said softly. "I had some, but I told Eli and he got my medicine from the car. He wore what he called his town gloves." She glanced at the door. "He said if he wasn't careful, he could transmit the disease just by paying for supplies. They all have to wear special gloves when they're in town."

"Yet they deliberately spread the disease to people like us," Blake said. He wiped everything he had typed and began again on a clean form. "YOU MUST ESCAPE! THERE'S AN EPIDEMIC BREWING HERE! WE MUST GIVE WARNING, GET TREATMENT!"

She was shaking her head again. God, why hadn't Meda sent Rane to him? Rane would be afraid, too, but that would not stop her.

"EVEN IF I FAIL," he typed, "YOU MUST TAKE THE CAR AND GO—OR WE COULD ALL DIE. DO YOU REMEMBER HOW TO START THE CAR WITHOUT THE KEY?"

She nodded.

"THEN GO! SEND BACK HELP. GIVE WARNING!"

Tears ran down her face, but she did not seem to notice them. He spoke aloud with painfully calculated brutality. "Meda told me people with serious injuries die of the disease. She's seen them die. She didn't say anything about people with serious illnesses, but Kerry, she didn't have to." He gave her a long look, trying to read her, reach her. She knew he was right. She wanted to please him. But she had to overcome her own fear.

He typed, "SOONER OR LATER, ELI WILL TOUCH YOU—AT LEAST."

She read the words without responding.

"BE NEAR THE WAGONEER TONIGHT," he typed. "AT TWO."

She swallowed, nodded once.

At that moment, there was a sound at the door. Instantly, Blake shut off the computer, automatically wiping the prescription form and everything he had typed. He closed the bag and turned to face the door just as Eli opened it.

Blake looked at Keira, aching to hug her. He felt he was about to lose her in one way or another, but he could not touch her.

PAST 9

Within twenty-four hours, Eli had infected everyone on the mountaintop ranch. He had also talked the old man, Gabriel Boyd, into giving him a job as a handyman. Boyd was not willing to pay much more than room and board, but room and board was all Eli really wanted—a chance to stay and perhaps save some of these people.

He was given a cot in a back room that had been used for storage. He was given his meals with the family, and he worked alongside the men of the family. He knew nothing about ranching or building houses, but he was strong and willing and quick. Also, he knew his Bible. This in particular impressed both the old man and his wife. Few people read the Bible now, except as literature. Religion was about as far out of fashion as it had ever been in the United States—a reaction against the intense religious feeling at the turn of the century. But Eli had been a boy preacher during that strange, not entirely sane time. He had been precocious and sincere, had read the Bible from Genesis to Revelation, and could still talk about it knowledgeably. Also, Eli knew how to be easygoing and personable, a refugee from the city, grateful to be away from the city. He knew how to win people over even as he condemned them to illness and possible death.

He wanted them all to start showing symptoms at about the same time, and he wanted that time to be soon. Left to themselves, infected people feeling their symptoms tended to huddle together in an us-against-the-world attitude. If everyone became ill at the same time, he would have less trouble keeping individuals from trying to go for help. He had started what could become an epidemic. Now, if he were going to be able to live with himself at all, he had to contain it.

He worked hard on the house that was intended for the son named Christian—Chris to everyone but his father. Christian's wife Gwyn was going to have a baby and Christian had decided that the house would be finished before the baby arrived. Eli did not know or care whether this was possible, but he liked Christian and Gwyn. He worried about what the disease might do to a pregnant woman and her child. Whatever happened would be his fault.

Sometimes guilt and fear rode him very nearly into insanity, and only the exhausting hard work of building kept him connected to the world outside himself. He liked these people. They were decent, kind, and in spite of the angry God they worshipped, they were remarkably peaceful and uncorrupted by the cynicism and violence outside. They were good people. Yet it was inevitable that some of them would die.

The daughter Meda was doing her best to add to his burdens by seducing him. She had no subtlety, did not attempt any.

"I'd like to sleep with you," she told him when she got her courage up. He had known since he met her that she wanted to sleep with someone, and would settle for him. He fended her off gently.

"Girl, what are you trying to do? Get yourself in trouble and get me shot? Your people have been good to me."

"They wouldn't," she said, "if I told them who you are. They think heaven is only for God and his chosen."

He became serious. "Don't play games with me, Meda. I like your honesty and I like you, but don't threaten me."

She grinned. "You know I wouldn't tell."

"I know."

"And if I can keep one secret, I can keep two." She touched his face. "I'm not going to let you alone."

Her touch produced an interesting tingle. She was coming into her time. He had apparently arrived just after her time of fertility the month before. That had been a blessing. He had been able to avoid the other two young women, but Meda would not let him avoid her. Now, she had no idea the trouble she was courting. She probably imagined a romantic interlude. She did not imagine being thrown on the rocky ground and hurt—inevitably hurt.

"No," he said, pushing her away. She was still smiling when he turned from her and began hammering in siding nails. She watched for a while, and he discovered he enjoyed the attention. He had not believed women outside the crew would want to look at him with his body so changed. Meda was trouble, but he was sorry when she decided to leave. She looked as though she had lost a little weight, he noticed.

As she walked away, her brother Christian came out of the main house and stopped her. They were too far from Eli to worry about his hearing them, but he heard every word.

"That guy been talking to you, Mead?" Christian demanded. Eli could not recall having heard Christian refer to him as "that guy" before. For Christian this was damned unfriendly.

"Sure he has," Meda said. "I came out here to talk to him. Why shouldn't he talk to me?" Blast her honesty!

"What'd you say to him?"

"What did you do this morning, Chris? Look in the mirror and mistake yourself for Dad?"

"What did he say to you?"

Eli looked at them and saw even over the distance that she smiled sadly. "Relax," she told her brother. "He said no. He said the family had been good to him and he didn't want trouble."

Christian gave an oddly brittle laugh. "Anybody who recognizes you as trouble has the right idea," he said. "If that guy were white, I'd tell you to marry him."

Meda watched her brother with visibly growing confusion.

Living in the house, Eli had heard enough to know Christian was
her favorite brother. They had shared secrets since childhood.
Christian knew how tired she was of being an isolated virgin, and
she knew how nervous he was about becoming a father. Right
now, she knew there was something wrong with him.

"Did you break down and buy some perfume?" he asked.
"You smell good."

Eli put down his hammer and stood up. It was beginning.
Meda had bathed and she smelled of soap, but she was not
wearing perfume. She was simply coming into her time. If she and
her brothers lived, they would have to learn to avoid each other
at these times. Now, however, Eli might have to help them. He
stood still, waiting to see whether Christian could control himself.
He realized Meda might not be as much in control as she should
be either. He would not let them commit incest. They would be
losing enough of their humanity shortly.

Eli jumped down from the floor of the house and started
toward them. At that moment, Christian reached up and touched
Meda's face with one trembling hand. Then, with a strange,
whining cry, he folded slowly to the ground, out cold.

PRESENT 10

When Eli and Keira were gone, Blake opened his bag and turned it on again. He punched in his identity code, then the words "TIMED SLEEP" and the number three. He hit the deliver button. Moments later, he had a capsule that would put him to sleep for three hours and let him awake fully alert. Next he ordered a much less precise dosage for Meda. This he ordered in injectable form—a sleep tab.

He placed Meda's dosage under the pillow he intended to use, then turned off the bag and closed it. He stripped to his shorts, and got into bed. Remembering Keira, he doubted that he could have slept at all without the capsule. And he had to sleep. If he did not, Meda would look at him and realize he was up to something. She might even figure out what it was. He did not underestimate her any longer.

He thought he heard her come in before he dozed off, thought she called his name. He may have muttered something before the drug took full effect.

He awakened on time, clearheaded, aware of what he must do. The room was full of moonlight and Meda lay snoring softly beside him. It amused him that she snored. It seemed utterly right that she should.

He was surprised to find himself feeling sorry for her as he eased the sleep tab from beneath his pillow and pressed it to her thin, bare right arm. She repelled him, but she was not responsible for what she had become.

There was no pain involved, but at his touch, she jumped, came awake, found him leaning over her.

"What did you do?" she demanded, fully alert.

He touched her hair, thinking he would have to hit her again, not wanting to hit her, not wanting to hurt her at all. Perhaps that was what she saw in his expression—if she could see him well enough to read his expression. She smiled uncertainly, turned her face to meet his caressing hand.

Then the smile vanished. "Oh God," she said. "What have you done?" She reached for him, but her hands had no strength. She tried to get up and almost slid out of bed. Finally the drug stopped her. She moaned and slipped into unconsciousness.

Blake stared at her, feeling irrationally guilty. He straightened her body, placed her in a more comfortable-looking position, and covered her. She would awaken in three or four hours.

He dressed, looked around the room, noticed at once that his bag was gone. He looked through the closet and in the bathroom, searched the bedroom, but the bag was not to be found. Finally, desperately, he forgot the bag and began searching for the key that would let him out of the room. Since he already knew where it was not, he began by searching the one place he had ignored: the bed and Meda herself. He found it on a chain around her neck. It hung down inside her gown where he could not have touched it normally without awakening her.

Seconds later, he let himself out of the room. Feeling his way carefully, silently, he reached the front door. He wondered just before he let himself out whether these people posted a watch. If they did, he was probably finished. He hoped they had enough confidence in their ability to handle their prisoners not to bother with guards.

He slipped out and closed the door behind him. From where he stood on the porch, he could see no one. Things looked confusingly different in the moonlight. For several seconds, he could not find the car. It had been moved. He feared it had been hidden and he would have to risk stealing another. Then he saw it in the distance near one of the outhouses. Getting it started without his key would be no problem if he had time to disconnect the trap-alarm system. The alarm itself was sound and indelible dye sprayed over any would-be thief. If the thief persisted, he was sprayed with a nausea gas. The gas was utterly disabling whether it was breathed or merely came in contact with the skin. A car —even a fuel-gulper like this one—was a prestige item. The automobile age had peaked and passed. People who drove cars or rode motorcycles now were either professional drivers, the rich, law-enforcement people, or parasites. The pros, the rich, and the police usually went to even greater, deadlier lengths than Blake had to protect their vehicles.

Hugging the shadows, Blake worked his way toward his car. He had reached it and used his own special catch to get past the hood lock when someone spoke to him.

"You don't have to do that. I have the keys."

He turned sharply, found himself facing Keira. Solemnly, she handed him his keys. He stared at them.

"I took them," she said. She shrugged. "Now you won't have to worry about touching me."

"You exposed yourself just to get the keys?" he demanded.

"No." She was in shadow. He could not see her well enough to be certain of her expression, but she sounded odd. He took the keys and her hand, held both for a moment, then hugged her tightly, probably painfully, though she did not complain. Then he held her by her shoulders and spoke what he strongly suspected was nonsense. "Meda says the disease is transmitted by inocula-tion, not contact. Don't touch your mouth or scratch your skin until you wash."

She did not seem to hear. "I hit him, Dad."

"Good. Get in the car."

"He had some books—made of paper, I mean—and an old bookend in the shape of an elephant. It was made of cast iron."

"Get in, Kerry!"

"I didn't want to hurt him. I didn't think I could hit him hard enough to do any real harm." She got in through the door he had opened.

He started to close the door, then instead squatted beside her. "Kerry, did you hear anything about Rane? Do you know where she is?"

"With Ingraham and Lupe. I don't know which house they're in."

She did not know. And how many people would he wake up if he tried to find out? One would be enough to recapture him. He had not even been bright enough to get himself another knife —not that the first one had done him any good. What he needed was a gun.

"Daddy, I heard something," Keira said.

He froze, listened, heard it himself—someone moving around carelessly in the house nearest to him. It may have been just someone going to the bathroom, but it frightened him. He rounded the car in a few long steps, got in, and heedless of noise, started the engine. At that moment, someone opened the door of the house from which the noise had come. It was a man, a stranger, who actually managed to catch the car as Blake swung it around toward the rocky trail that led down from the ranch. The stranger tried to tear Blake's door open as Ingraham had earlier. But with the car moving and his body inadequately braced, he failed to break the lock. He was dragged several yards as Blake picked up speed. As a final gesture, he managed to release his hold with one hand, raise his fist, and smash it into the window beside Blake's head. Like the lock, the glass held. It broke, cracks raying outward in all directions from the impact of the blow, but it did not shatter. Its breaking amazed Blake. The glass was special, expected to stop bullets with less damage. Blake realized again how powerful these people were. If they caught him, they could literally tear him limb from limb.

He drove on, praying that he would see Rane, that he would have a chance to pick her up. But he saw only stick people— menacing, utterly terrifying in their difference and their intensity. In the moonlight, they seemed other than human. One refused to move from the car's path, apparently trying to make Blake swerve and hit a house or a huge rock.

Blake did not swerve. No experienced city driver would have swerved or slowed. At the last possible instant, the "victim" leaped aside and clung to the rock like an insect.

Something that moved like a cat, but was too big to be a cat, ran alongside the car briefly, and Keira screamed.

"Don't hit him," she said. "Don't hurt him!"

The car accelerated, leaving the running thing behind.

"What the hell was that?" Blake asked.

"Be careful," she said. "Remember the rocks Eli had to dodge around."

He remembered. It was impossible to speed past those boulders. On the other hand, it was very possible that Meda's people in the mountains above could start rockslides that would close the narrow road entirely if he crept along slowly.

As though in answer to his thought, he heard a rumbling from above. Praying as he had not since childhood, he drove on, managed to swerve around one boulder just in time to see a rockslide beginning ahead.

He pushed the accelerator to the floor, sped past the slide area as the first rocks came down. Twice the car was hit by rocks big enough to shake it, but Blake managed to stay on the road. He did not slow down until he came to a sharp curve around which he thought he recalled a rock.

There was a rock. Many rocks. Another slide had blocked the road with a steep hill of loose rocks and dirt. Blake had no time to think. The car would climb the slide or it would not. It was a Jeep, after all, antique or no.

The car struggled for traction in the loose dirt and rock, then shuddered heavily as something landed on its roof. The something made an indentation they could see inside the car.

Suddenly Keira pushed her door open. Blake grabbed for her, not understanding. His hand just missed her as she leaned out. Then he saw what she had seen—a small, bloody face hanging upside down from the cartop.

"Rane!" he shouted. He leaned across Keira, indifferent for

the moment to the way Keira bruised almost at a touch. He caught Rane's arm, pulled her down and into the car across Keira, then slammed the door and locked it as something else began tearing at it.

Blake hit the accelerator and the car leaped onto the loose dirt and rock. For an instant, the wheels spun uselessly, throwing out sand. Then they found traction and the car lunged up the slide. A rock bounced off the windshield, chipping it slightly. Another hit the top, doing no important damage.

Blake reached the crest of the slide, rolled down it, and sped on down the mountain. Minutes later, they were in open desert. Keira and Rane, still tangled together, both hurting, both silent with terror until they looked around and saw that they had left the mountains and their captivity behind. Then they hugged each other, Rane laughing and Keira crying. Rane's bare arms and her face had been cut and bruised somehow. If she had not been contaminated before, she was now. Blake worried, but said nothing. Contamination had probably been inevitable from the moment of capture. Its effects did not have to be inevitable, however. The disease could be studied, understood, stopped, or at least controlled—and it had to be. The disease was only a disease. It was the willing human carriers intent on spreading it that made it so deadly.

Blake relaxed in his seat and surveyed the damage to the car. Nothing terminal. Nothing that would stop him from reaching civilization and getting medical care. He wondered why Eli's people had not shot him, or at least shot at him. Bullets would have been more effective than rocks. But then, it was like Eli to hold back. He had saved Rane from Ingraham, held off contaminating Keira—probably for as long as he could—even tried bloodlessly to avoid a fight with Blake, though he could probably have broken Blake's bones with no effort.

"How did you get free?" Keira was asking Rane. "Did you have to hurt someone?"

"I was tied up for the night," Rane said. "Jacob let me loose. He didn't like me, but he couldn't stand the thought of anything being tied up. Then you two broke away and everyone was too busy chasing you to watch me. I almost killed myself running and falling down that goddamn mountain."

"Jacob?" Blake said. "Isn't that one of Meda's sons?"

The girls looked at each other, then at him warily. "You know about Jacob?" Rane asked.

"Only that Meda has a son by that name."

"He's her son and Eli's." There was an odd pause. For the second time in twenty-four hours, Rane seemed unwilling to say what was on her mind. "Have you seen him?" she asked.

"No. But I don't imagine he would be normal. Not after what the bag told me about Meda."

". . . he isn't."

"What's he like?"

"You saw him," Keira said softly. "He ran alongside the car for a few seconds. That was him."

Blake frowned, gave her a quick glance. "But that was . . . an animal."

"Disease-induced mutation. Every child born to them after they get the disease is mutated that way. Jacob is the oldest of eleven."

Blake glanced at Keira. She was not looking at him, would not look at him.

"Jacob's beautiful, really," she continued. "The way he moves—catlike, smooth, graceful, very fast. And he's as bright as or brighter than any other kid his age. He's—"

"Not human," Blake said flatly. "Jesus, what are they breeding back there?"

The girls looked at each other again, shifted uncomfortably, sharing some understanding that excluded him. Now neither would face him. Suddenly he wanted to be excluded. He drove on in silence, suspicion growing in his mind. He concentrated on putting distance between himself and those who would certainly follow—though he could not help wondering whether what followed was really worse than what they carried with them.

PART 2

P. O. W.

Within a day of Christian's collapse, Eli had seven irrational people huddling around him. They had no idea what was happening to them, but they knew they were in trouble. They were combative, fearful, confused, lustful, driven, guilt-ridden, and utterly miserable.

They huddled together, not knowing what to do. They were fearful of going near outsiders with their painfully enhanced senses and their odd compulsions, but Eli was one of them. More, he was complete. He smelled *right* to them. And he could see their needs clearer than they could. He could respond to them as they required, offering comfort, sternness, advice, brute strength, whatever was necessary from moment to moment.

He found comfort in shepherding them. It was as though in a very real way, he was making them his family—a family with ugly problems.

Meda found both her brothers and her father after her, and she, like them, was alternately lustful and horrified. Her father suffered more than the others. He felt he had gone from patriarch and man of God to criminally depraved pervert unable to keep his hands off his own daughter. Nor could he accept these feelings as his own. They must be signs of either demonic possession or God's punishment for some terrible sin. He and his sons were badly frightened.

His wife and daughters-in-law were terrified. Not only were they unable to understand the behavior of their men, but they were confused and embarrassed by their own enhanced sensory awareness. They could smell the men and each other as they never had before. They kept trying to wash away normal scents that would not vanish. They spoke more softly as they realized the substantial walls no longer stopped sound as well as they had. They discovered they were able to see in the dark—whether they wanted to or not. Touching, even accidentally, became a startlingly intense sensual experience. The women ceased to touch each other. They also ceased to touch the men except for their own husbands. And Eli.

They all developed huge appetites as their bodies changed. Worse, they developed unusual tastes, and this frightened them.

"I'm so hungry," Gwyn told Eli on the day her symptoms became undeniable. She gestured toward a pair of chickens—part of the Boyd flock of thousands. This pair were scratching and pecking at the sand in the shade of the well tank. "Suddenly, those things smell good to me," she said. "Can you believe that? They smell edible."

"They are," Eli said softly. It had been necessary for him to supplement his diet with one or two of them or with several eggs every night when the family was asleep.

"But how could they smell good raw?" Gwyn said. "And alive?"

Living prey smelled wonderful, Eli knew. But Gwyn was not ready to face that yet. "Go raid the refrigerator," he told her. "Maybe Junior is hungry."

She looked down at her pregnant belly and tried to smile, but she was clearly frightened.

He did what he would never have done before this day. He took her arm and led her back to the house to the kitchen. There he saw to it that she ate. She seemed to appreciate the attention.

"Something feels wrong," she said once. "Not with the baby," she added quickly when Eli looked alarmed. "I don't know. The food tastes too sweet or too salty or too spicy or too something. It tasted okay yesterday, but now . . . When I started to eat, I thought I was going to be sick. But that's not right either. It's not really nauseating. It's just . . . I don't know."

"Bad?" he asked, knowing the answer.

"Not really. Just different." She shook her head, picked up a piece of cold fried chicken. "This is okay, but I'm not sure the ones running around outside wouldn't be better."

Eli said nothing. Since his return to Earth, he knew he preferred his food raw and unseasoned. It tasted better. Yet he would go on eating cooked food. It was a human thing that he clung to. His changed body seemed able to digest almost anything. It tempted him by making nonhuman behavior pleasurable, but most of the time, it let him decide, let him choose to cling to as much of his humanity as he could.

Though certain drives at certain times inevitably went out of control.

Meda brought him her symptoms and her suspicions not long after he left Gwyn.

"This is your doing," she said. "Everybody's crazy except you. You've done something to us."

"Yes," he admitted, breathing in the scent of her. She had some idea now what she was doing to him just by coming near.

"What have you done?" she demanded.

"What do you feel?" he asked, facing her.

She blinked, turned away frightened. "What have you done?" she repeated.

"It's a disease." He took a deep breath. He had never imagined that telling her would be easy. He had already decided to be as straightforward as possible. "It's an extraterrestrial disease. It will change you, but no more than I'm changed."

"A disease?" She frowned. "You came back sick and gave us a disease? Did you know you had it?"

"Yes."

"And you knew we could catch it?"

He nodded.

"Then you gave it to us deliberately!"

"No, not deliberately."

"But if you knew . . ."

"Meda . . ." He wanted to touch her, take her by the shoulders and reassure her. But if he began to touch her, he would not be able to stop. "Meda, you'll be all right. I'll take care of you. I stayed to take care of you."

"You came here to give us a disease!"

"No!" He turned his head toward the well tank. "No, I came . . . to get water and food."

"But you—"

"I couldn't die. I wanted to, but I couldn't. I can go out of my mind; I can become an animal; but I can't kill myself."

"What about the others, the crew?"

"All dead like I told you, like your Barstow news said. The disease took some of them—before we found out how to help them." A half-truth. A deletion. Disa and two others had died in spite of the help they got. "The others died here—with the ship. Someone—maybe more than one—apparently managed a little sabotage. I wish they'd done it in space, or back on Proxi Two."

"How do you know someone sabotaged the ship? Maybe it was an accident."

"I don't know. I don't remember. I blacked out."

"How did you get off the ship?"

"I don't know. I have off-and-on memories of running, hiding. I know I took shelter in mountains of volcanic rock, lived in a half-collapsed lava tunnel for three days and two nights. I nearly starved to death."

"People can't starve in just three days."

"We can. You and me, now."

She only stared at him.

"It was raining," he continued. "I remember we deliberately chose to land in a storm in the middle of nowhere so we could get away before anyone found out what we were. Even with speeded up reflexes, increased strength, and enhanced senses, we nearly disintegrated, then nearly crashed. We kept them from shooting us down by talking. God, we talked. The brave heros giving all the information they could before they crashed. Before they died. We could no more imagine ourselves dying than we could imagine not coming straight in to Earth. It was a magnet for us in more ways than one. All those people . . . all those . . . billions of uninfected people."

"You came to infect . . . everybody?" she whispered.

"We *had* to come. We couldn't not come; it was impossible. But we thought we could control it once we were here. We thought we could take only a few people at a time. A few isolated people. That's why we chose such an empty place."

"Why would you think you could have any . . . any luck controlling yourselves here in the middle of all the billions if you couldn't control yourselves on Proxima Centauri Two?"

"We weren't sure," he said. "Maybe it was just something we told ourselves to keep from going completely crazy. On the other hand . . ." He looked at her, glad she was alive and well enough to be her questioning, demanding self. "On the other hand, maybe we were right. I don't want to leave this place to reach anyone else. Not now. Not yet."

"You've done enough damage here."

"Do you want to leave?"

"Eli, I live here!"

"Doesn't matter. Do you want to go to a hospital? See if somebody can figure out a cure?"

She looked uncomfortable, a little frightened. "I was wondering why you didn't do that."

"I can't. Can you?"

"What do you mean you can't?"

"Go if you can. I'll . . . try not to stop you. I'll try."

"This is my home! I don't have to go anywhere!"

"Meda—"

"Why don't *you* leave! You're the cause of all this! You're the problem!"

"Shall I go, Meda?"

Silence. He had frightened and confused her, touched a brand new tender spot that she might not have discovered on her own for a while. She wanted to stay with her own kind. Being alone was terrifying, mind-numbing, he knew.

"You went away," she said, reading him unconsciously. "You left the rest of the crew."

"Not deliberately."

"Do you ever do anything deliberately?" She came a little closer to him. "You got out. Only you."

He realized where she was headed and did not want to hear her, but she continued.

"The one sure way you could have known when to run is if you were the saboteur."

His hands gripped each other. If they had gripped anything else at that moment, they would have crushed it. "Do you think I haven't thought about that?" he said. "I've tried to remember."

"If I were you, I wouldn't want to remember."

"But I've tried. Not that it makes any difference in the end. The others died and I should have died. If I did it, I killed my friends then made their deaths meaningless. If someone else did it, my survival made the sacrifice meaningless anyway."

"The dogs died," she said. "Remember? One of them was hurt, but not bad. The other wasn't hurt at all, but they died. We couldn't understand it."

"I'm sorry."

"They *died!* Maybe we'll die!"

"You won't die. I'll take care of you."

She touched his face, finally, traced the few premature lines there. "You aren't sure," she said. "My touch hurts you, doesn't it?"

He said nothing. His body had gone rigid. Its center, its focus was where her fingers caressed.

"It must hurt you to hold back," she said. "Your holding back hurts me." There were agonizing seconds of silence. "You probably were the saboteur," she said. "You're strong enough to hurt yourself, so you thought you were strong enough to kill yourself. I want you. But I wish you had succeeded. I wish you had died."

He had no more strength of will at all. He seized her, dragged her behind the well, pushed her to the ground. She was not surprised, did not struggle. In fact, with her own drives compelling her, she helped him.

But it was not only passion or physical pain that caused her to scratch and tear at his body with her nails.

PRESENT 12

When Orel Ingraham grasped Rane's arm and led her from Meda's house, she held her terror at bay by planning her escape. She would go either with her father and Keira or without them. If she had to leave them behind, she would send help back to them. She had no idea which law enforcement group policed this wilderness area, but she would find out. All that mattered now was escaping. Living long enough to escape, and escaping.

She was terrified of Ingraham, certain that he was crazy, that he would kill her if she were not careful. If she committed herself to a poorly planned escape attempt and he caught her, he would certainly kill her.

She noticed no trembling in the hand that held her arm. There were no facial tics now, no trembling anywhere. She did not know whether that was a good sign or not, but it comforted her. It made him seem more normal, less dangerous.

As they walked, she looked around, memorizing the placement of the animal pens, the houses, the large chicken house, and something that was probably a barn. The buildings and large rocks could be excellent hiding places.

The people were spooky; she saw only a few, all adults. They were busy feeding the animals, gardening, repairing tools. One woman sat in front of a house, cleaning a chicken. Rane watched with interest. She planned to be a doctor eventually, and was pleased that the sight did not repel her. What did repel her was the way people looked at her. Each person she passed paused for a moment to stare at her. They were all scrawny and their eyes seemed larger than normal in their gaunt faces. They looked at her with hunger or lust. They looked so intently she felt as though they had reached for her with their thin fingers. She could imagine them all grabbing her.

At one point, an animal whizzed past—something lean and brown and catlike, running at a startling speed. It was much bigger than a housecat. Rane stared after it, wondering what it had been.

"Show-off," Ingraham muttered. But he was smiling. The smile made him look years younger, less intense, saner. Rane dared to question him.

"What was that?" she asked.

"Jacob," Ingraham answered. "Stark naked as usual."

"Naked?" Rane said, frowning. "What was it?"

He led her onto the porch of an unpainted, but otherwise complete, wooden house. There he stopped her. "Not 'it,' " he said, "him. That was one of Meda's kids. No, shut up and listen!"

Rane closed her mouth, swallowing her protests. But the running thing had definitely not been a child.

"Our kids look like that," he said. "You may as well get used to it because yours are going to look like that too. It's a disease that we have, and now you have it—or you'll soon get it. There isn't a damn thing you can do about it."

With no further explanation, he took her into the house and turned her over to a tall, pregnant woman whose hair was almost long enough for her to trip over.

Lupe, the woman's name was. She was sharp-featured with thin arms and legs. In spite of her pregnancy, she clearly belonged among these people. She wore a caftan much like Keira's. Her pregnant belly looked like a balloon beneath it. She reached for Rane with thin, grasping hands.

Rane drew back, but Ingraham still held her. She could not escape. The woman caught Rane's other arm and held it in a grip just short of painful. The thinness was deceptive. These people were all abnormally strong.

"Don't be afraid," the woman said with a slight accent. "We have to touch you, but we won't hurt you." Her voice was the friendliest thing Rane had heard since her capture. Rane tried to relax, tried to trust the friendly voice.

"Why do you have to touch me?" she asked.

"Because you're not one of us yet," Lupe said. "You will be. Be still." She reached up so quickly that Rane had no chance to struggle, and made scratches across Rane's left cheek.

Rane squealed in surprise and pain, and, too late, jerked her head back. "What did you do that for?" she demanded.

They ignored her. "You're in a hurry," Ingraham said to Lupe.

"Eli says the sooner the better with this one and her father," Lupe told him.

"While he takes his time with his. Treats her like she'll break if he touches her."

"She might. We never had anybody who was already sick."

"Yeah. I got us a healthy one, though."

They talked about her as though she were not there, Rane thought. Or as though she were no more than an animal who could not understand.

She tried to pull free when Lupe took her away from Ingraham and sat her down on a long wooden bench. There, finally, she released Rane and stood before her studying Rane's angry, hostile posture. Lupe shook her head.

"I lied," she told Rane. "We are going to hurt you. You're going to fight us every chance you get, aren't you? You're going to make us hurt you." The corners of her mouth turned downward. "Too bad. I can tell you from experience, it won't help. It might kill you."

Rane glanced at the woman's claws and said nothing. Lupe was as crazy as Ingraham and even more unpredictable with her soft words and sharp nails. Rane was terrified of her—and furious at her for inspiring fear. Why should one thin-limbed, pregnant woman be so frightening? One thin-limbed, startlingly strong, pregnant woman who sat down beside Rane and caressed Rane's arm absently.

Rane looked at Ingraham—actually found herself looking for help from the man who had held a gun to her head. To her utter humiliation, he laughed. Rane's vision blurred and for an instant, she saw herself smashing his head with a rock.

Suddenly Lupe grasped her chin, turned her head until she could see only Lupe, hear only Lupe.

"*Chica*, nothing has ever truly hurt you before," Lupe said. "Nothing has even threatened you enough to make you believe you could die. Not even your sister's illness. So now you must learn a hard lesson very quickly. No, don't say anything yet. Just listen. You think I'm threatening you, but I'm not. At least, not in the way you believe. We have given you a disease that can kill you. That's what you need to understand. Some of our differences are signs of that disease. You must decide whether it's better to live with such signs or die. Listen."

Rane listened. She heard about Eli and the *Clay's Ark* and Proxima Centauri Two. She listened, but she believed almost nothing.

"You know," Lupe said when she had been talking for perhaps a half hour, "sometimes I look around and everything seems to be the wrong color. The sun is too bright and . . . not red. I feel surprised that it isn't red. I couldn't figure out what was going on when it first happened. It scared me. But when I told Eli, he said Proxi was red. A cool red star with its three planets hugging in close around it. He bought some red light bulbs in Needles and put them in his den. They're not right either, really, but every now and then I go over there. Every now and then, everyone goes over there and stays for a while. It relaxes us. When things start to smell funny to you and you feel like you want to eat a live rabbit or rape a man, we'll take you over there. It helps. Keeps you from jumping out of your skin."

"I've got a better solution for that last feeling," Ingraham said, grinning. He had gone away and come back. Now he sat watching Rane in a way that made her nervous. In spite of the huge meal Rane had seen him eat, he was munching nuts from a dish on the coffee table.

Lupe looked at him and smiled—all teeth. "You touch her like that and I'll cut your thing off."

Ingraham laughed, got up and kissed her, then stood before her, smiling. "You want me to get one of the kids for her to see?"

"Get Jacob if you can catch up with him."

"Okay." He went out.

Looking after him, Rane sorted out two impressions. First, that Lupe meant her threat absolutely. She would kill him if she caught him with Rane or any other woman. Second, he knew it. He enjoyed her possessiveness. Thus Rane was probably safe from him in one way at least. Thank God.

"You're bright," Lupe said to her softly. "Very bright, but stubborn. You think you can choose your realities. You can't."

Rane made herself meet the woman's eyes. "Reality," she said with contempt. "My father is a doctor. He really could have gone out on the *Ark*. He has valuable training, he was within the age range when it left, and he was in good physical shape. Would you believe me if I told you he was a fugitive astronaut?"

"Not if you're his kid, honey. Nobody with young kids went. No white guy married to a black woman went either. Things never got that loose."

"And no ignorant con artist who can barely speak English went," Rane snapped. "If Eli's convinced you he did, you're no smarter than he is!"

Surprisingly, Lupe smiled. "You're a lot less tolerant than I would have expected. A lot less observant too. But it doesn't matter. Here's Jacob."

Ingraham came into the room carrying a small, large-eyed, brown boy. The boy was slender—without childish pudginess—but not bone-thin like the adults. He wore a pair of blue shorts, but no shirt. He was startlingly beautiful, Rane realized when he turned in Ingraham's arms and faced her. But there was something odd about him. He seemed nothing like the thing that had run past her outside, but he did appear to be built for speed. An odd, slender little boy.

"Come on, *niño,*" Lupe said. "Let's show you off a little bit. Come sit with us."

The boy scrambled against Ingraham, braced, and leaped to the bench on which Rane and Lupe sat. He landed next to Rane, who started violently. Jacob had leaped like a cat and landed on all fours. His legs and arms were clearly intended to be used this way. He was a quadruped. He had hands, however, and fingers. He looked at them, following Rane's eyes.

"They work," he said in a clear, slightly deeper than average child's voice. "They work like yours." He grasped her arm with the small, startlingly strong, hard hands. Sharp little nails dug into her flesh, and she drew away. Squatting, the boy sniffed his hands, then wiped them on his shorts.

"You smell," he told Rane, and leaped off the bench and onto it again next to Lupe.

Lupe laughed. "Shame, Jacob. That's not nice to say."

"She does," the boy insisted.

"She's not one of us yet. She will be soon. Then she'll smell different."

Rane completely passed over the insult in her fascination with the boy—the whatever-it-was.

"Can he walk on his feet alone?" she asked Lupe.

"Not so well," Lupe answered. "He tries sometimes because we all do, but it's not natural to him. He gets tired, even sore if he keeps at it. And it's too slow for him. You like to move fast, don't you, *niño?*" She lifted the strange little body and placed it on her lap. Jacob immediately put his ear to her belly.

"I can hear it," he announced.

"Hear the baby?" Rane asked.

"Its heartbeat," Lupe said. "He can hear it without putting his ear to me. It's just a game he likes. He says this one's going to be a girl. He doesn't understand how he can tell, but he knows. Smell, maybe."

"Guessing, maybe," Rane said.

"Oh no, he does know. He's called it right four times so far. Now women come and ask him."

"But . . . but, Lupe—"

"Stop for a moment," Lupe said. Then to the boy, "Okay, niño. Back out to play. Take some nuts."

The boy leaped down from her lap, trotted on all fours to the china nut dish on the plain, homemade coffee table. He took a handful of nuts, stuffed them into the pocket of his shorts and zipped it shut. He seemed to have no trouble using his hands. They were smaller than Rane thought they should have been, but he was less clumsy with them than a normal child would have been. He was certainly much faster than any normal child, probably faster than most adults. All his movements were smooth and graceful. A graceful four-year-old.

He stopped in front of her—beautiful child head, sleek cat-like body. A miniature sphinx. What would it be when it grew up? Not a man, certainly.

"I don't like you either," Jacob said. "You're fat and you smell and you're ugly!"

"Jacob!" Lupe stood up and started toward him. "*Vayase! Ahora mismo!* Outside!"

Jacob bounded out the door. No, human beings did not move that way. How had any disease made such a creature of a child?

"He's telling the truth, you know," Lupe said. "You do look fat and odd to him, though you're not. And you smell . . . different. Also, he couldn't miss how much you were repelled by him."

"I don't understand how such a thing could happen," Rane whispered.

"It's the disease, I told you. We don't even have a name for it—the disease of *Clay's Ark*. All our children are like Jacob."

"All . . . ?" Rane swallowed. "All animals? All *things?*"

"Shit!" Lupe said. "You're worse than I was. You should be more tolerant. He's a little boy."

Rane stared at her pregnant belly.

"Oh yes," Lupe said. "This child will be like Jacob too, just as my son is. Beautiful and different. And, *chica*, your children will be like him too. The disease doesn't go away. It just settles in and stays with you and you pass it on to strangers and to your children."

"Or you get treatment!" Rane said. "What the hell are you doing sitting in the middle of the desert giving birth to monsters and kidnapping people?"

Lupe smiled. "Eli says we're preserving humanity. I agree with him. We are. Our own humanity and everyone else's because we let people alone. We isolate ourselves as much as we can, and the people outside stay alive and healthy—most of them."

"Most," Rane said with bitterness. "Most for now. But even now, not me. Not my father or sister. And what about you? You don't belong here either, do you?"

"I do now," Lupe said. "Before, I was a private hauler. You know. Good money if you survive. My truck broke down all the way over on I-Fifteen, and Eli caught me outside. When I realized what he had done to me, I thought I would bide my time and kill him. Now, I think I'd kill anyone who tried to hurt him. He's family."

"Why?" demanded Rane. "If you really believe he's the cause of this sickness—and you know he's the guy who kidnapped you . . ." Rane shook her head. "Didn't you have a husband or anything back in the real world? What about your business?"

"I was divorced," Lupe said. "I lived in the truck on the road." She paused. Her voice became wistful. "I miss the road. I almost got killed more times than I like to think about, but I miss it."

Rane listened without comprehension. A woman who could be nostalgic for work that kept nearly killing her could probably make any irrational adjustment.

"I didn't have anybody," Lupe said. "We lived in a cesspool. My parents' house got caught in a gang war, got bombed. One of the gangs wanted to make a no-man's-land, you know. They needed to put some space between their territory and their rivals'. So they bombed some houses, torched others. They got their no-man's-land. My parents, my brother, and a lot of other people got killed. My ex-husband, he's a wino somewhere. Who cares? So I was alone. I'm not alone here. I'm part of something, and it feels good. Even Orel. There was a time when I carried two guns plus the truck's usual defenses—and defensively, my truck was a goddamn tank—all to fight off people like him: bike packers, car bums, rogue truckers, every slimy maggot crawling over what's left of the highway system. But they're not all as bad as I thought. Orel isn't. Take away the gang and give him something better and he turns into a person. A man."

Rane listened with interest in spite of herself. She could not understand Lupe's interest in a man like Ingraham but she was beginning to respect Lupe. Rane liked to think of herself as tough, but she had an uncomfortable suspicion she could not have survived Lupe's life. She had never been alone, never been without someone who would help her if she could not help herself. Now none of the people who cared about her could help her. Her father, her sister, two sets of grandparents, and on her mother's side, a number of aunts, uncles, and cousins. Only a few of them were close to her, but every one of them could be counted on to come running if a member of the family needed help. Now, the only ones who knew of her need needed help as badly as she did.

PAST 13

Gabriel Boyd died.

Death was a relief to him, an end to more than physical suffering. Alive, he was frightened, confused, full of self-loathing for feelings he could neither control nor understand.

He had had to be put to bed because he was no longer able to keep his balance. He overcompensated, first for walking up and down steps, then for negotiating the irregularities of the ground outside, finally for walking over a level surface. He could crawl, but nothing more.

As his sensitivity increased, he began to react with terror to slight sounds and cringe at the slightest touch. Most food—even the smell of food—nauseated him, though he was always hungry. Eli fed him ground, unseasoned raw meat, fresh vegetables, and fruit. He ate a little of this and kept it down.

His eyes had to be covered since any slight movement frightened him. His movements, even in bed, were either exaggerated and awkward or fine and incredibly controlled. He could no longer feed himself. Then he could no longer eat or drink even if fed. On the *Ark*, he would have been fed intravenously. But no member of the *Ark* crew who reached this stage had survived, reinfection or no. Eli and a weeping Meda cared for him, then for his wife, whose symptoms also worsened. He lost control of all his bodily functions. He urinated and defecated, spat and drooled. His body twitched and convulsed and sweated profusely. He probably shed enough disease organisms to contaminate a city.

On the fourth day following the onset of symptoms, he died —probably of dehydration and exhaustion. On life support, he would have lasted longer, but the end would have been the same. Eli was glad there were no facilities for prolonging the old man's suffering.

Meda's mother died a day later as did her two brothers and a tiny, perfectly formed nephew born three months too soon.

Meda herself never really sickened. She became more and more despondent as her family died, became almost suicidal, but her physical symptoms remained bearable. She was learning to use her enhanced senses or at least tolerate them. And in spite of all the horror, every night and sometimes during the day, she went to Eli or he came to her. Without discussion, he moved into her room. She did not understand how she could touch him with the disaster he had brought to her family happening all around her. Yet she found comfort with him. And, though she did not know it, she gave him comfort, eased his guilt simply by continuing to live. They leaned on each other desperately, and somehow held each other up.

Her father realized what they were doing before he died. He first cursed her, called her a harlot. Then he apologized and wept. He seized Eli's wrist with only a ghost of the great strength he should have possessed.

"Take care of her!" he whispered. It was more a command than a request. Even more softly, he said, "I know it might have been me or one of her brothers if not for you. Take care of her, please."

To Eli's own surprise, he wept. He was trapped in a vise of guilt and grief. He was alive because of the old man. Gabriel Boyd had given him a home and thus kept him from drifting into a town and spreading the disease. It was his grandfather all over again—a stern, godly old man who took in strays. A dangerous practice these days—taking in strays.

He worried about Meda. Worried that he might not be able to take care of her—that she might die in spite of her apparent adjustment. That would make him a complete failure. That would drive him away even if her sisters-in-law lived. In his mind, only her living would ease his questioning of his own humanity. He had stayed to save her. Now she must live or he was a monster, utterly evil, completely without control of the thing that made him monstrous.

She lived. He stayed with her constantly during the period when she might try to take her life. Later when the organism took firmer hold, suicide would be impossible. Now, he watched her.

Most of the time she hated him at least as much as she needed him. She lost weight and her clothing sagged on her. She gained strength, and when she hit him, it hurt. Guiltily, he did not strike back.

She helped him wash the corpses of her parents, her brothers, and her nephew. For him it was a penance he would not permit himself to avoid. For her it was a good-bye.

They wrapped the bodies in clean sheets, took them to a place she had chosen. There, together, they broke the ground, dug the graves. The sisters-in-law did not help, but they crept out to stand red-eyed over the graves as Eli read from Lamentations and from Job. They cried and Meda said a prayer and it was over.

Later, Meda tried to comfort her sisters-in-law. They were older than she, but she had a more dominant personality, and they tended to defer to her—except in one important way. They preferred to be comforted by Eli. Their drives were as much increased as Meda's and they had no men.

Meda understood their need, but resented it. Even when she hated Eli, she did not want to share him. Her possessiveness seemed to surprise her, but it did not surprise Eli. He would have been equally possessive of her if there had been another man on the ranch. He saw to it that Gwyn and Lorene were reinfected until he was certain they would live. Then he avoided temptation as best he could until Meda was comfortably pregnant—and her pregnancy did comfort her. She did not understand why. She had been isolated and sheltered by her parents, brought up to believe having a child outside marriage was a great sin. But her pregnancy relieved tension she had not recognized until it was gone. It also relieved tension she had recognized all too clearly.

"I'm going to sleep with Lorene," Eli told her one day. "It's her time."

Meda rubbed her stomach and looked at him. "I don't want you to," she said. He could see that she meant the words, but he heard little passion behind them. She had some idea what he was feeling, and she knew positively what Lorene was feeling. She wanted to hold on to him, but she had already resigned herself to his going.

"There are no other men," he said unnecessarily.

"Will you come back?"

"Yes!" he said at once. Then more tentatively, "Shall I?"

"Yes!" she said matching his tone. She put her hand to her stomach. "This is your child too!"

She did not know how much he wanted to be a father to it. He had been afraid she would do what she could to make that difficult.

"We need men for Lorene and Gwyn," she said.

He nodded. He was glad she had said it. She would share the responsibility this time when they infected two more men. He had known all along what had to be done. He had not thought the women were ready to hear it until now. The other deaths had seemed too fresh in their minds. Without meaning to, he had enjoyed the harem feeling the three women gave him. When he realized how much he enjoyed it, he wanted to look for other men at once. He found any feeling that would have been repugnant before his illness, but that was now attractive, to be suspect. He would not give the organism another fragment of himself, of his humanity. He would not let it make him a stud with three mares. He would make a colony, an enclave on the ranch. A human gathering, not a herd. A gathering headed where, God knew, but wherever they were headed, since they were not going to die, they had to grow.

PRESENT 14

Lupe and Ingraham shared Rane with a newcomer introduced as Stephen Kaneshiro. No one explained what he was doing
there. He offered to help with the wall painting when Lupe and
Ingraham got out the paint and brushes—real brushes—but Rane
did not get the impression he lived with them. He touched her
from time to time as Lupe and Ingraham did. After a couple of
hours of this, she stopped cringing and trying to avoid their
fingers. They were not hurting her. There was no more scratching. They were endurable.

Eventually the reason for Stephen's presence became clear
to her.

The painting had been going on for a while when Lupe asked
her if she wanted to help. She shook her head. She knew the
request might really be a command, but she decided to wait and
see. Lupe simply shrugged and turned back to the wall she was
working on. The two men were on their way to work on the
outside of the house. Stephen stopped, looked at her, then at
Lupe. "Do you suppose she'll be this lazy when she has her own
house?" he asked.

Lupe smiled. "That one isn't lazy. She's sitting there cooking
up an escape plan."

Startled, Rane turned to look at her. Lupe laughed, but Stephen seemed concerned. He put down a can of paint and came over to Rane. He was a small, brown man, so heavily tanned that he and Rane were about the same color. He was clean-shaven and long-haired, his black hair pulled back and loosely bound with a rubber band. Under different circumstances, she would have welcomed attention from him, even been a little overwhelmed. He was as thin as everyone else on the ranch, but he was also one of the best-looking men Rane had ever seen. Somehow, his thinness did not detract from his good looks. Yet he had the disease. She braced herself against the renewed offense of his touch.

But this time he did not touch her. He clearly wanted to, but he held back.

"If you'll come with me," he said, "I won't touch you."

"Do I have a choice?" she asked.

"Yes, but I'd like you to come. I want to talk to you."

Rane glanced at Lupe, saw that she was paying no attention. Stephen did not seem fearsome. He was her size and not afflicted with any twitches or trembling. She sensed none of Ingraham's quick temper behind the quiet, black eyes. More important, she was learning absolutely nothing sitting in Lupe's living room and being stroked like an animal whenever someone thought of her. She needed to look around, find a way out of this place.

She stood up, looked at Stephen, waiting for him to lead the way.

"We're going outside," he said. "I'll show you around while we talk. Don't run, though. If you run, I'll have to hurt you—and that's the last thing I'd want to do."

There was no special warmth in his voice when he said these last words, but Rane was suddenly suspicious.

Breaking his word, Stephen took her arm and led her out. She did not mind, really. At least this time he had a reason to touch her.

He took her to a corral where two cows and a half-grown heifer were eating hay. Far off to one side, there was another corral from which a bull stared at the cows.

"This place is full of babies and pregnant women," he said.

"We need plenty of milk." The heifer came over to them and he rubbed its broad face.

"You can get a disease from drinking raw milk," Rane said.

"We know that. We're careful—although we're not sure we have to be. We don't seem to get other diseases once we have this one."

"It's not worth it!"

He looked surprised at her vehemence. "Rane, you'll be all right. Young women don't have anything to worry about. It's older women and all men who take the risk."

"So I've heard. That means my father could die. And, young or not, my sister will probably die sooner than she would have without you people. And me. What do I do if I live? Give birth to one little animal after another?"

He turned her around so that she faced him. "Our children are not animals!" he said. "We are not interested in hearing them called animals."

She pulled free of him, not at all surprised that he let her. "I never cared much for the idea of aborting children," she said, "but if I thought for a moment that I was carrying another Jacob, I'd be willing to abort it with an old wire coat hanger!"

She had managed to horrify him—which was what she had intended. She was completely serious, and he, of all people, had to know it.

"You know they planned to give you to me," he said softly.

"I suspected. So I wanted you to know how I felt."

"Your feelings will change. Ours did. The disease changes you."

"Makes you like having four-legged kids?"

"Makes you like having kids. Makes you need to have them. And when they come, you love them. I wonder . . . What's the chemical composition of love? Human babies are ugly even when they're normal, but we love them. If we didn't the species would die. Our babies here—well, if we didn't love them, if we weren't damned protective of them, the *Clay's Ark* organism on Earth would die. It isn't intelligent, but, God, is it ever built to survive."

"I won't change," Rane said.

He smiled and shook his head. "You're a strong girl, but you don't know what you're talking about." He paused. "You don't have to come to me until you want to. We're not rapists here. And you . . . Well, you're interesting right now, but not as interesting as you will be."

"What are you talking about?"

He put his arm around her. She was surprised that the gesture did not offend her. "You'll find out eventually. For now, it doesn't matter."

They walked away from the heifer and she mooed after them.

"Cows don't seem to get the disease," he commented. "Dogs get it and it kills them. It kills all the types of cold-blooded things that have bitten us—snakes, scorpions, insects . . . There may not be anything on Earth that can penetrate our flesh and come away unchanged. Except our own kind, of course. I can't prove it, but I'll bet those cows are carriers."

"The scope attachment of my father's bag could probably tell you that," Rane said. "Though he may not be in any mood to use it."

"I can use it," he said.

She looked at his face, lineless in spite of his thinness. He was the youngest person she had seen so far—in his early twenties, perhaps, or his late teens. "You were in school before, weren't you," she guessed.

He nodded. "College. Music major. I got a little sidetracked taking biology and chemistry classes, though."

"What were you going to be?"

"A concert violinist. I've been playing since I was four."

"And now you're willing to give it all up and move back to the twentieth century?"

He stopped at a large wooden bin, opened it, and watched as a couple of dozen chickens came running and gathered around, clucking. He opened one of the six large metal barrels, took out a handful of cracked corn, and threw it to them. This was clearly what they were waiting for. They began pecking up the corn quickly before the newcomers who came in from every direction could take it from them. Stephen threw a little more of the corn, then closed the bin.

"It's almost sunset," he said. "You'd think they'd be too busy deciding where they were going to roost to watch the bin."

"Don't you care that you're never going to be a musician?" she demanded.

He looked down at his hands, rubbed them together. "Yes."

His voice had dropped low into his own private pain. She stood silent, feeling awkward, for once not knowing what to say. Then he looked up at her, smiled faintly. "It was an old passion," he said. "I haven't touched a violin for months. I didn't know what that would be like."

"What is it like?" she asked.

He began to walk so that she almost missed his answer. "An amputation," he whispered.

She walked with him, let him lead her out to the garden, passing the Wagoneer on the way. The sight of it jarred her, reminded her that she should be watching for a way of escape.

"Did you ever see food growing?" he asked, bending to turn a deep green watermelon over and look at its yellow bottom. "Ripe," he commented. "You wouldn't believe how sweet they are." He was distracting. He moved from one subject to another, drawing her with him, keeping her emotionally involved in whatever he chose.

"I don't care about food growing," she said. "Listen, Stephen, my father is a good doctor. Let him examine you—maybe the disease can be cured. If he can't help you himself, he'll know who can."

"We don't leave the ranch," he said, "except to bring in supplies and converts."

"You'll never be a violinist here!"

"I'll never be a violinist," he said. "Don't you think I know that?" He never raised his voice. His expression changed only slightly. But she felt as though he had shouted at her. She watched him with fascination.

"Why?" she asked. "What's holding you here?"

"I belong here. These are my people now."

"Why? Because they gave you a disease?"

"Yes."

"That doesn't make sense!" she said angrily.

"It will."

His apparent passivity infuriated her. "You were probably nothing as a violinist. You probably didn't have anything to lose. That's why you don't care!"

His face froze over. "If you want to get rid of me," he said, "go on saying things like that."

In that moment, she realized she did not want to get rid of him. He seemed human and the others did not. Just a few minutes with him had made her want to cling to him and avoid the stick people and animal children who were her alternative. But she would *not* cling to him. She would not cling to anyone.

"I don't care what you do," she said. "I don't understand why anyone would want to stay here, and you haven't said anything to help me understand."

"Nothing I say would really help." He sighed. "When your symptoms start, you'll understand. That's all. But try this. I was married. My wife played the piano—played it maybe better than I played the violin. We had a son who was only a year old when I saw him last. If I stay here, my wife can go on playing the piano. The world will go on being a place where people have time for music and beauty. My son can grow up and do whatever he wants to. My parents have some money. They'll see that he has his chance. But if I try to turn myself in, I know I'll lose control and spread the disease. I would begin the process of turning the world into a place with no time for anything but survival. In the end, Jacob and his kind would inherit everything. My son . . . might never live to be a man."

She was silent for several seconds when he finished. She found herself wanting to say something comforting, and that was insane. "You've sacrificed my family to spare yours," she said bitterly.

He pulled an ear of corn from its stalk, husked it, and began eating it raw. He tore at it like an animal, not looking at her.

"Someone sacrificed you, too," she said finally. "I know that.

But Jesus, isn't it time to break the chain? You and I could get away together. We could get help."

"You haven't heard me," he said. "I knew you wouldn't. Listen! We're infectious for as much as two weeks before we start to show symptoms—except for people like you who won't have two weeks between infection and symptoms. How many people do you think the average person could infect in two weeks of city life? How many could his victims infect?—and with an extraterrestrial organism. There's no cure, Rane, and by the time one is found—if one can be found—it will probably be too late. It isn't only my family I'm protecting. It's everyone. It's the future. As Eli told me, the organism is a damned efficient invader."

"I don't believe you!"

"I know. Nobody believes it at first. I didn't."

Rane walked away from him as he picked a tomato and began to eat. He never washed anything. Ate them just as they grew out of the dirt. Rane had never seen food growing this way before, but it did not impress her. She wondered whether they fertilized it with the contents of the outhouse and the animal pens. It was just the sort of filthy anachronistic thing they might do.

She climbed some rocks—huge, rough rounded mounds of granite—and stood on top, staring down. To her surprise, she saw the road winding below. Then Stephen was beside her. She started violently to find him there in a space that had been empty a second before. He must have leaped up, almost the way Jacob would leap.

"We can all jump," he said. "We can run pretty fast, too. You should remember that."

"I wasn't trying to get away."

"Not yet. But remember anyway." He paused. "Do you know how they caught me seven months ago?"

"You've only been here seven months?"

"I drove right into their settlement," he said. "I'd gone to see my folks in Albuquerque and on my way home, I decided to do some exploring. I discovered a mountain road that wasn't on my maps, and thought I'd find out where it led. I found out."

"Why were you driving?" Rane asked. "You should have flown."

"I loved to drive. It was a kind of hobby. I'll bet your father has the same affliction."

"Yeah. He has a Porsche and a Mercedes at home. He won't even drive them outside the enclave."

"A Porsche? You're kidding. What year?"

She looked at him, saw excitement on his face for the first time and laughed. Something familiar at last. Car craziness. "1982 Porsche 930 Turbo. My mother used to call it his other wife. My sister and I figured it was his other kid."

He laughed, too, then sobered. "It's getting dark, Rane. We should go in."

She did not want to go in—back to Lupe and Ingraham. Back to hands that made her cringe. Stephen's hands did not make her cringe any longer.

"I don't have a house, yet," he said. "I have a room in Meda's house."

She could not look at him now. She had never slept with a man. The thought of doing so now with a stranger—even a likable stranger confused and frightened her. The thought of conceiving a child in this place—if you could call them children—terrified her.

"Back to Lupe, then," he said. He put his arm around her, and startled her by snatching her up and jumping off the rocks. They landed safe and unhurt amid stalks of corn. She thought she weighed at least as much as he did, but her weight did not seem to bother him.

"You're not a screamer," he said. "Good." He set her on her feet.

"Am I like your wife?" she asked timidly as they walked back.

"No," he answered.

"But . . . do you like me?"

"Yes."

She looked at him uncertainly, wondering if he were laughing at her. "I wish you talked more," she said.

* * *

Later that night, Lupe tied Rane to a bed.

"We don't have bars yet," Ingraham said. "You should have gone with Stephen."

"Shut up," Lupe told him. "Tying people up is no joke. Neither is trying to send a kid to bed with a guy she doesn't even know. We gotta find a better way. I'm sick of this."

Ingraham said nothing more.

Rane found no comfort in Lupe's sentiment. Tied as she was, she had to ask even to go to the bathroom. And she could not sleep on her side as was her custom. She lay miserable and sleepless, twisting her wrists in the hope of freeing at least one. The twisting hurt enough to make her stop after a while. Then she tried to reach one of her wrists with her teeth. And failed.

By then she was crying tears of frustration and anger. She was totally unprepared for the sudden weight across her stomach that knocked the breath out of her. This time she would have screamed if she had been able to.

She caught her breath, feeling as though she had been punched, then saw Jacob dim and shadowy in the darkness above her.

"You can't bite the rope," he said. "Your teeth are too dull."

"What are you doing here?" she demanded.

"Nothing." He stared down at her from the pose of a seated cat. "I came in the window."

Rane sighed, closed her eyes. "I think I'm glad you're here," she whispered. "Even you."

"Why don't you like me?" he demanded.

She shook her head, answered honestly because she was too tired to humor him. "Because you look different. Because I'm afraid of you."

"You are? Of me?" He sounded pleased. He also sounded closer. She opened her eyes and saw that he had stretched out beside her. She tried to draw away, but could not.

"You *are* afraid of me," he said gleefully. "I'm going to sleep here."

She could have called Lupe. She made a conscious decision not to. The boy was harmless in spite of his appearance, and he did not understand that what she feared was not him personally, but what he represented. Most important, she did not think she could stand to be alone again.

Sometime after midnight, when she had developed a headache from lack of sleep, he awoke and with unchildlike alertness, asked if her arms hurt.

"They hurt," she said. "And I can't sleep and I'm cold."

To her surprise, he pulled her blankets up to her chin. "Bikers put a rope on me," he said. "They pulled me and said, 'Heel, heel!' "

Rane shook her head in disgust. Jacob could not help what he was. He did not deserve such treatment.

"Daddy hit some of them and they died."

"Good for him," Rane muttered. Then she realized she was talking about Eli, who might even now be raping Keira. Confusion, frustration, and weariness set in heavily, and she could not stop the tears. She made no sound, but somehow, the child knew. He touched her face with one of his hard little hands, and when she turned her head away angrily, he turned his attention to her right wrist.

"What are you doing?" she demanded.

As though in answer, she found her wrist suddenly free.

"My teeth are sharp," Jacob announced. He climbed over her and started on her left wrist. In seconds, it too was free.

"Oh God," she said, hugging herself with aching arms and numb hands. She made herself reach out to the child. "Thank you, Jacob."

"You taste good," he said. "I thought you would. You smell like food."

She drew her hand back quickly, heard his gleeful laugh. Let him laugh. He had freed her. How the hell a four year old could have teeth that cut rope was beyond her, but she didn't care. If he had been a little less strange, she would have hugged him.

"Something is happening outside," he said.

"What?"

"People moving around and talking." He bounded off the

bed and to the window. "They're your people," he said. He leaped silently to the high window sill, then down the other side.

Then even she heard the noise outside—a car starting, people running. There was shouting, and finally what must be happening penetrated her weary mind. Her people—her father and sister . . .

She got out of bed, taking time only to slip into her shoes and grab her pants and shirt. She threw both on over the thin gown Lupe had brought her from her luggage and she went through the window. She would have climbed through it naked if she had had to.

She got out in time to see the Wagoneer disappearing down the mountain road, stick people in hot pursuit. Her father had left her!

She took a few useless steps after them, then turned without conscious thought and ran in the opposite direction—toward the rocks she and Stephen Kaneshiro had stood on. Toward the road below where her father would almost certainly be passing soon. It occurred to her as she headed for the steep incline that she could be killed. The thought did not slow her. Either way, the stick people would not tie her down again.

PART 3

MANNA

Now Eli would become an active criminal as well as the carrier of a disease. Now, with the help of Lorene and Meda, he would abduct a man. He would take Meda's father's Ford and go to what was left of old U.S. 95. Meda knew 95 from State Highway 62 to Interstate 40. It was desolate country, she said. No towns, almost no private haulers on the road. Just a few daredevil sightseers, taking their chances among the bike packs and car families, and a few well-armed, individualistic ranchers.

Eli worried about taking Meda along. She was four months pregnant, and he worried about both her and the child. She was not an easy woman to become attached to, but the attachment had happened. Now he could not lose her. *He could not lose her.*

Meda had always been physically strong, had taken pride in being able to match her brothers at hard work and hard play. Now the disease had made her even stronger, and her new strength had made her overconfident.

She would not, she told Eli, sit at home, trembling and wondering whether her child's father had survived. She intended to see that he survived—and, he thought, maybe get herself killed in the process.

Eli swung from anger to amusement to secret gratitude for her concern. There were still bad times with her—times when she cursed him and mourned her family. But these times came less frequently. Both the disease organism and the child inside her were driving her toward him. Perhaps she had even begun to forgive him a little.

Now she helped him plan.

"We can hide here," she said, using an old paper auto club map. "There's a junction. A dirt road runs into Ninety-five. There are some hills."

All four of them sat clustered at one end of the large dining room table. Lorene, who was to have the new man if he lived; Gwyn, who was already pregnant again and in less immediate need of a man of her own; Meda; and Eli.

Covertly, Eli watched Gwyn, saw that she seemed at ease, uninterested in the map. A few weeks before, she would have torn the yellowed paper in her eagerness to take part and get a man for herself. Now, pregnant by Eli, she was content. The organism had turned them all into breeding animals.

"What do you think?" Meda asked him.

He looked at the map. "Damn lonely stretch of road," he said. "Anyone working here?" He pointed to a quarry that should have been nearby.

Meda shook her head. "Too dangerous. What this highway really is at that point is a sewer. From what I've heard about city sewers, the only reason they're worse is because they have more sewer rats. But the gangs here are just as dangerous, and the haulers . . . body-parts dealers, arms smugglers—that kind. The few holdout ranchers are dangerous too. If they don't know you, they shoot on sight."

"Dangerous," Eli said. "And close. Too close to us here. I used to see lights from Ninety-five when I went out at night." When he went out to kill and eat chickens to supplement Meda's mother's idea of three good meals. "I think I saw lights from State Highway Sixty-two, too. If we accidentally catch anyone important, I don't want search parties coming right to us."

Meda gave a short, bitter laugh. "People disappear out here all the time, Eli. It's expected. And nobody's important enough these days to search this country for."

Eli glanced up from the map and smiled. "I am. Or I would be if anyone knew I was alive."

"Come on," she said, irritated, "you know what I mean."

"Yeah. I hear bike gangs and car families can be damned vindictive, though, if they think you've hurt one of theirs. Let's go up to I-Forty. If things are bad there, we could even go on to I-Fifteen."

"That far?" Meda said. "Fuel, Eli."

"No problem. We'll take the Ford. With its twin tanks it can go just about anywhere within reason and come back without a fill-up."

"And there are more people on Forty and Fifteen," Lorene said. "Real people, not just sewer rats. I could get an honest hauler or a farmer or a city man." She sounded like an eager child listing Christmas possibilities. In a moment, Eli would have to make her hear herself. Left on her own, she could do a lot of harm before she realized what was happening to her.

"The Ford's been to Victorville and back without fuel problems," Gwyn said lazily. She was from Victorville, Eli knew. Christian had met her there, where she had worked with her brothers at their mother's roadside station. She shrugged. "I don't think we'll have a fuel problem."

Meda looked at her strangely, probably because of her lazy tone, then spoke to Eli. "I assume you want to use Ninety-five for going and coming."

"We can use it for going," he said. "If you think it's worth the detour."

She shook her head. "Car families set up roadblocks. Armored tour buses and private haulers just bull their way through, but cars get caught. Especially one car alone."

"We'll use this network of dirt roads, then. I like them better anyway. You know the best ones?"

She nodded. "In good weather, some of them are smoother than Ninety-five, anyway."

"And the dirt roads will give captives the idea they're more isolated than they are. They won't be able to prowl around and find out the truth the way I did until they've made it through the crisis period. After that, they won't care."

"Are you sure they won't?" Meda asked. "I mean . . . this is our home, but some stranger . . ."

"This will be his home."

Lorene giggled. "I'll make him feel at home. You just catch him."

Eli turned to look at her.

"You know," she said, still laughing, "this is the kind of

thing you always read about men doing to women—kidnapping them, then the women getting to like the idea. I think I'm going to enjoy reversing things."

Silence. Meda and Gwyn sat staring at Lorene, clearly repelled.

"We won't touch him," Eli told Lorene. "We'll leave it to you to give him the disease."

Lorene's smile vanished. She looked from Meda and Gwyn to Eli.

"He might die on you," Eli continued. "If he does, we'll get you another one."

She frowned as though she did not understand.

"We'll get you as many as necessary," he said.

"You don't have any right to make me feel guilty!" she whispered. Her voice rose abruptly. "This is all your fault! My husband—"

"Remember him!" Eli said. "Remember how it felt to lose him. Chances are, you'll be taking someone else's husband soon."

"You have no right—"

"No, I don't," he said. "But then, there isn't anyone else to say these things to you. And you have to hear them. You have to understand what you are—why you feel what you feel."

"It's because you killed—"

"No. Listen, Lori. It's because you're the host, the vehicle of an extraterrestrial organism. It's because that organism needs new hosts, new vehicles. You need to infect a man and have children and you won't get any peace until you do. I understand that. God knows I understand it. The organism is a damned efficient invader. Five people died because I couldn't fight it. Now, it's possible that at least one person will die because you can't fight it."

"No," Lorene whispered, shaking her head.

"It's something we can't forget or ignore," Eli continued. "We've lost part of our humanity. We can lose more without even realizing it. All we have to do is forget what we carry, and what it needs." He paused. She had turned away, and he waited until she faced him again. "So we'll get you a man," he said. "And we'll turn him over to you. You'll give him the disease and you'll care for him. If he dies, you'll bury him."

Lorene got up and stumbled out of the room.

PRESENT 16

When Blake and Meda had gone, when Ingraham had led Rane away, Eli and Keira sat alone at the large dining room table. Keira looked across at Eli bleakly.

"My sister," she whispered. Rane had looked so frozen when Ingraham led her out, so terrified.

"She'll be all right," Eli said. "She's tough."

Keira shook her head. "People think that. She needs to have them think that."

He smiled. "I know. I should have said she's strong. Maybe stronger than even she knows."

A woman carrying a crying child of about three years came into the house. The child, Keira could see, was a little girl wearing only underpants. She had a beautiful face and a dark, shaggy head of hair. There was something wrong with the way she sat on the woman's arm, though—something Keira could not help noticing, yet could not quite identify.

The woman smiled wearily at Eli. "Red room," she said. Eli nodded.

The woman stared at Keira for a moment. Keira thought she stared hungrily. When she had gone into a room off the living room and shut the long, sliding door, Keira faced Eli.

"What's going on?" she said. "Tell me."

He looked at her hungrily, too, but then leaned back in his chair and told her. No more hints, no more delays. When he finished, she asked questions and he answered them. At one point, the woman and child came out of the red room and Eli called them to him.

"Lorene, bring Zera over. I want you both to meet Kerry."

The woman, blond and thin, came over with her hungry eyes and her strange child. She looked at Keira, then at Eli. "Why is there still a table between you two?" she asked. "I'll bet there's no table between that guy and Meda."

"Is that what I called you over here for?" he asked, annoyed. "Don't you want to brag about your kid a little?"

Lorene faced Keira almost hostilely.

Keira and the child had been staring at each other. Keira roused herself, met Lorene's suspicious eyes. "I'd like to see her."

"You see her," Lorene said. "She's no freak. She's supposed to be this way. They're all this way."

"I know," Keira said. "Eli has told me. She's beautiful."

Lorene put her daughter on the table and the child immediately sat down, catlike, arms braced against the floor.

"Stand up," Lorene said, pushing at the little girl's hindquarters. "Let the lady see you."

"No!" Zera said firmly. To Keira, that proved something about her was normal. Before Keira's illness, she had been called on to take care of little toddler cousins who sometimes seemed not to know any other word.

Then Zera did get up, and in a single fluid motion, she launched herself at Eli. He seemed to pluck her out of the air, laughing as he caught her.

"Little girl, I'm going to miss some day. You're getting faster."

"What would happen if you did miss?" Keira asked. "She wouldn't hurt herself, would she?"

"No, she'd be okay. Lands on her feet like a cat. Lorene does miss sometimes."

"I never miss," Lorene said, offended. "I just step aside sometimes. I'm not always in the mood to be jumped on."

Eli put Zera back on the table and this time, she walked a few steps, leaped off the table, and stood beside Lorene.

Keira smiled, enjoying the child's smooth, catlike way of moving. Then she frowned. "A kid that age should be kind of clumsy and weak. How can she be so coordinated?"

"We've talked about that," Eli said. "They do go through a clumsy period, of course. Last year, Zee fell down all the time. But if you think she's agile now, you should see Jacob. He's four."

"What will they be like when they're adults?"

"We don't know," Lorene said softly. "Maybe they peak early—or maybe they're going to be as fast as cheetahs some day. Sometimes we're afraid for them."

Keira nodded, looked at the child. She was perfect. A perfect, lean, little four-legged thing with shaggy uncombed hair and a beautiful little face. "A baby sphinx," Keira said, smiling.

"Think you could handle having one like this someday?"

Keira glanced at her, smiled sadly, then turned back to Zera. "I think I could handle it," she said.

Zera took a few steps toward her. Keira knew that if the child scratched or bit her, she would get the disease. Yet she could not bring herself to be afraid. The child was as strange a being as Keira had ever seen, but she was a child. Keira reached out to her, but Zera drew back.

"Hey," Keira said softly. "What do you have to be afraid of?" She smiled. "Come here."

The little girl mirrored the smile tentatively, edged toward Keira again. She was a little cat not sure it should trust the strange hand. She even sniffed without getting quite close enough to touch.

"Do I smell good?" Keira asked.

"Meat!" the child said loudly.

Startled, Keira drew back. She expected to be scratched or bitten eventually, but she did not want to have to shake Zera off her fingers. Anything as sleek and catlike as this child probably had sharp teeth.

"Zee!" Lorene said. "Don't bite!"

Zera looked back at her and grinned, then faced Keira. "I don't bite."

The teeth did look sharp, but Keira decided to trust her. She started to reach out again, this time to lift the child into her lap, but Eli spoke up.

"Kerry!"

She looked across the table at him.

"No."

His voice made her think of a warning rattle. She drew back, not frightened, but wondering what was wrong with him.

Lorene seemed angry. She picked up Zera and faced Eli. "What kind of game are you playing?" she demanded. "What's the kid here for? Decoration?"

Eli looked up at her.

"Don't give me that look. Go do what you're supposed to do. Then you can take care of her! And if she doesn't make it, you can—"

Eli was on his feet, inches from her, looming over her. Keira held her breath, certain he would hit the woman and perhaps by accident, hurt the child.

Lorene stood her ground. "You're soaking wet," she said calmly. "You're putting yourself through hell. Why?"

He seemed to sag. He touched Lorene's face, then Zera's shaggy head. "You two get the hell out of here, will you?"

"What is it!" Lorene insisted.

"Leukemia," Eli said.

There was silence for a moment. Then Lorene sighed. "Oh." She shook her head. "Oh shit." She turned and walked away.

When she had gone through the front door, Keira spoke to Eli. "What are you going to do?" she asked.

He said nothing.

"If you touch me," she said, "how soon will I die?"

"It isn't touch."

"I know. I mean—"

"You might live."

"You don't think so."

More silence.

"I'm not afraid," she said. "I don't know why I'm not, but . . . You should have let me play with Zera. She wouldn't have known and Lorene wouldn't have cared."

"Don't tell me what I ought to do."

She could not fear him—not even when he wanted her to. "Is Zera your daughter?"

"No. She calls me Daddy, though. Her father's dead."

"You have kids?"

"Oh yes."

"I always thought someday I'd like to."

"You've prepared yourself to die, haven't you?"

She shrugged. "Can anyone, really?"

"I can't. To me, talking about it is like talking about the reality of elves and gnomes." He smiled wryly. "If the organism were intelligent, I'd say it didn't believe in death."

"But it will kill me."

He got up, pushing his chair away angrily. "Come on!"

He led her into the hall and to a large bedroom. "I'm going to lock you in," he said. "The windows are locked, but I guess even you could kick them out if you wanted to. If you do, don't expect any consideration from the people you meet outside."

She only looked at him.

Abruptly, he turned and left the room, slamming the door behind him.

Keira lay down on the bed feeling listless, not quite in pain, but unable to worry about Eli, his guilt, the compulsion that would surely overcome him soon. Her body was warning her. If she did not get her medication soon, she would feel worse. She closed her eyes, hoping to fall asleep. She had the beginnings of a headache, or what felt like the beginnings of one. Sometimes the dull, threatening discomfort could go on for hours without really turning into a headache. She rolled over, away from the wet place her sweating body had made. *Clay's Ark* victims were not the only people who could sweat profusely without heat. Her joints hurt her when she moved.

She had decided she was to be left alone for the night when Eli came in. She could see him vaguely outlined in the moonlight. Apparently, he could see her much better.

"Fool," he said. "Why didn't you tell me you felt bad? You've got medicine in the car, haven't you?"

Not caring whether he could see or not, she nodded.

"I thought so. Get up. Come show me where it is."

She did not feel like moving at all, but she got up and followed him out. In the dining room, she watched him pull on a pair of black, cloth-lined, plastic gloves.

"Town gloves," he said. "People take us for bikers in stores sometimes. I had a guy serve me once with a shotgun next to him. Damn fool. I could have had the gun anytime I wanted it. And all the while I was protecting him from the disease."

Why are you protecting me? she thought, but she said nothing. She followed him out to the car, which had been moved farther from the house. There, she showed him the compartment that contained her medicine. She had left it on the seat once, not thinking, and someone had nearly managed to smash into the car to get it, no doubt hoping for drugs. They would have been disappointed. They might have gotten into her chemotherapy medicines and made themselves thoroughly sick.

"Where's your father's bag?" Eli asked.

She was startled, but she hid her surprise. "Why do you want it?"

"He wants it. Meda says she's going to let him examine her."

"Why?"

"He wants to. It gives him the feeling he's doing something significant, something familiar that he can control. Knowing Meda, I suspect he needs something like that right now."

"Can I see him?"

"Later, maybe. Where's the bag?"

This time, she couldn't help glancing toward the bag's compartment. It was only a tiny glance. She did not think he had seen it. But he went straight to the compartment, located the hidden keyhole, stared at it for a moment, then selected the right key on the first try.

"You never turn on any lights," Keira said. "Does the disease help you see in the dark?"

"Yes." He took the bag from its compartment. "Take your medicine to your room. All of it."

"The bag won't work for you," she said. "It's coded. Only my father can use it."

He just smiled.

She had to suppress an impulse to touch him. The feeling surprised her and she stood looking at him until he turned abruptly and strode away. She watched him, realizing he may have felt as bad as she did. His smile had dissolved into a pinched, half-starved look before he turned away.

She stood where she was, first looking after him, then looking up at the clear black sky with its vast spray of stars. The desert sky at night was fascinating and calming to her. She knew she should follow Eli, but she stayed, wondering which of the countless stars was Proxima Centauri—or rather, which was Alpha Centauri. She knew that Proxima could not be seen separately by the unaided eye. A red star whose light a little girl born on Earth longed for.

"Hi," a child's voice said from somewhere nearby.

Keira jumped, then looked around. At her feet stood a sphinxlike boy somewhat larger than Zera.

"Daddy said you have to come in," the boy said.

"Is Eli your daddy?"

"Yes. I'm Jacob."

"Does anyone call you Jake?"

"No."

"Lucky boy. I'm Keira—no matter what you hear anyone else say. Okay?"

"Okay. You have to come in."

"I'm coming."

The boy walked beside her companionably. "You're nicer than the other one," he said.

"Other one?"

"Like you, but not as brown."

"Rane? My sister?"

"Is she your sister?"

"Where is she? Where did you see her?"

"She didn't like me."

"Jacob, where did you see her?"

"Do you like me?"

"At the moment, no." She stopped and stooped to bring herself closer to eye level with him. Her joints did not care much for the gesture. "Jacob, tell me where my sister is."

"You do like me," he said. "But I think Daddy will get mad at me if I tell you."

"Damn right, he will," Eli's voice said.

Keira looked up, saw him, and stood up, wondering how anyone could move so silently in sand that crunched underfoot. The boy moved that way, too.

"Eli, why can't I know where my sister is?" she asked. "What's happening to her?"

Eli seemed to ignore her, spoke to his son. "Hey, little boy, come on up here."

He did not bend at all, but Jacob leaped into his arms. Then the boy turned to look down at Keira.

"You tell Kerry what her sister was doing last time you saw her," Eli said.

The boy frowned. "Keira?"

"Yes. Tell her."

"You should call her Keira. That's what she likes."

"Do you?" Eli asked her.

"Yes! Now will you please tell me about Rane?"

"She was with Stephen," Jacob said. "They looked at the cows and fed the chickens and Stephen ate some stuff in the garden. Stephen jumped with her and she didn't like it."

"Jumped?" Keira said.

"From some rocks. She liked him."

Keira looked at Eli, questioning.

"Stephen Kaneshiro is our bachelor," Eli said, heading for the house again. Keira followed automatically. "He saw the two of you and asked about you. I aimed him at Rane."

"And she likes him."

"I'd say so. This little kid reads people pretty clearly."

"Is she with him?"

"She could have been. Stephen said it was too soon for her, so she's alone. Kerry, she's all right, I promise you. Beyond infecting her, no one wants to hurt her."

"Keira," Jacob said into Eli's ear.

Eli laughed. "Yeah," he said. He looked at the boy. "You know it's time for you to go to bed. Past time."

"Mom already put me to bed."

"I figured she had. What'll it take to get you to stay there?"

Jacob grinned and said nothing.

"The kids are more nocturnal than we are," Eli said. "We try to adjust them more to our hours for their own protection. They don't realize the danger they're in when they roam around at night."

He held the door open for her and she went in. "There are bobcats in these mountains, aren't there?" she asked. "And coyotes?"

"Jacob's in no danger from animals," Eli said. "His senses are keener than those of the big animals and he's fast. He's literally poison to most of the smaller ones—especially those that are supposed to be poison to him. No, it's the stray humans out there that I worry about." He stopped, looked at his son who was listening somberly. "Keira, you take your medicine, then go back to your room. There are some books in there if you want to read. I'm going to put this one to bed."

She obeyed, never thinking there might be anything else she could do. She caught herself feeling grateful to him for not hurting her, not even forcing the disease on her, though she didn't know how long that could last. Then she realized she was feeling gratitude to a man who had kidnapped her family. Her problem was she liked him. She wondered who Jacob's mother was. Meda? If so, why was Meda trying so hard, so obviously to get Blake Maslin into her bed. Perhaps he was there now. No, Jacob's mother must be someone else. She sat staring at the cover of a battered old book—something from the 1960s—written even before the birth of her father: *Ishi, Last of his Tribe.* She had intended to read, but she had no concentration. Finally, Eli appeared again to take her to her father.

That meeting was terrible. It forced her to remember that her liking for Eli could not matter. The fact that she was not afraid for herself could not matter. She had a duty to help her father and Rane to escape—and that terrified her. She did not underestimate the capacity of Eli's people to do harm. Her escape, her family's escape would endanger their families. They would kill to prevent that. Or perhaps they would only injure her badly and keep her with them in agony. She had had enough of pain.

But she had a duty.

"I shouldn't have let you see him," Eli said.

She jumped. She had been walking slowly back to her room, forgetting he was behind her. "I wish you hadn't," she whispered. Then she realized what she had said, and she was too ashamed to do anything but go into her room and try to shut the door.

He would not let the door shut.

"I thought it would be a kindness," he said, "to both of you." And as though to explain: "I liked the way you got along with Jacob and Zera. They're good kids, but the reactions they get sometimes from new people . . ."

She knew about ugly reactions. Probably Jacob knew more, or would learn more, but walking down a city street between her mother and her father had taught her quite a bit.

She reached out and took Eli's hands. She had been wanting to do that for so long. The hands first pulled back from her, but did not pull away. They were callused, hard, very warm. How insane to expose herself to the disease now that she knew she must at least try to escape. Yet she almost certainly already had it. Eli and her father had deluded themselves into believing otherwise, but she knew her own particular therapy-induced sensitivity to infection. Her father knew it too, whether or not he chose to admit it.

The hands closed on her hands, giving in finally, and in spite of everything, she smiled.

PAST 17

Ironically, Eli, Meda, and Lorene interrupted someone else's attempted abduction. Off Interstate 40, they found a car family or a fragment of a car family raiding a roadside station. There were few stations in the open desert these days. They offered water, food, fuels from hydrogen to fast-charge for electric cars, vehicle repairs, and even a few rooms for tourists.

"Stations help everyone," Meda said as they watched the fighting. "Even the rat packs usually leave them alone."

"Not this time," Eli said. "Hell, this isn't our fight. Let's see if I can get us out of here."

He could not. The Ford had apparently been spotted. Now, as Eli swung it around, the car people began to shoot at it. The Ford's light armor and bulletproof windows were hit several times, harmlessly. The bullet that hit the left front tire should have been equally harmless. Instead, the tire exploded. At the same moment, a high-suspension, tough Tien Shan pickup came across the sand from the station to cut the Ford off. They could not get back to the highway.

Eli stopped the Ford, and grabbed Gabriel Boyd's old AR-15 semiautomatic rifle. It wasn't the newest of old Boyd's collection of antiques, but Eli liked it. He slipped off the safety, and looked the Tien Shan over. Its too-large, crudely cut gunports presented the best targets. He aimed through one of the Ford's own custom crafted gunports. The Tien Shan's big openings were bull's-eyes. The barrel that emerged from one of them seemed to move in slow motion.

Eli fired. The rifle barrel in the Tien Shan jerked. Eli fired twice more, rapidly. The barrel in the Tien Shan slid backward, stopped, then remained still, pointed upward. Eli held back his last two rounds, waiting to see what would happen.

The Tien Shan sat silent. An instant later, Meda fired her rifle. Eli looked around, saw a man fall only a few feet from the Ford. On the opposite side of the car, Lorene fired her husband's rifle at a nearby rise. At first, it seemed she had done nothing more than kick up a puff of dust. Then a woman staggered from concealment, arms raised, one hand clutching her rifle by its barrel. As they watched, she fell face down into the sand.

Meda, who had probably been the best shot of the three of them before the disease, took aim at one of the other cars. She fired.

Again, nothing seemed to happen, but Eli swung the Ford around and charged the two cars. He had literally seen the bullet go through a window that was slightly open. And he could see through the tinted glass of that window well enough to know that Meda had made another kill. Others in the car had apparently had enough. The car turned and fled into the desert, followed by the third, unscathed vehicle.

"Amateurs!" Meda muttered, watching them go. "Why'd they have to come to us to get themself killed?"

Eli glanced at her, saw that she was actually angry at the car family for forcing her to kill. She was almost crying.

"Idiots!" she said. "Big holes cut for shooting! Open windows! Kids!"

"Probably," Eli said, reaching for her hand. She avoided

him, would not look at him. "What they were doesn't matter," he said. "They meant to kill us. We stopped them."

"You should be glad they were amateurs," Lorene told her. "If they were more experienced and better equipped, they would have killed us."

Eli shook his head. "I doubt it. We don't die that easily. And did you notice not one of them got off a shot at us after they blew our tire?"

"Yeah," Meda said. "Amateurs!"

"More than that," Eli told her. "We scared the hell out of them. We moved so fast we seemed to be anticipating them. If they're amateurs, they must have thought we were pros." He sighed. "Whoever's in the station might think that, too, so I don't think we'd better hang around here to change that tire."

"A stationmaster, Eli," Lorene said hungrily. "A station man."

He glanced at her. "Maybe it's a station woman or a family like Gwyn's."

"We could see."

"No, Meda's right about these places. They help everyone. We might need them more than most people eventually. No sense closing this one down."

To their surprise, the stationmaster ended their argument for them by poking his head out the station door, then stepping out and making a perfect target of himself.

"I don't believe this," Meda said.

"He's crazy," Eli said. "He doesn't know what we might be —and he doesn't know whether there's anyone left alive in the Tien Shan."

Meda shook her head. "Well, he'll find out for us."

The man drew no fire. He went to the Tien Shan and looked into the cab. He smiled at what he saw there—which must have taken a strong stomach and strong hatred.

"I don't think he's the stationmaster," Eli said. "Stationmasters can be tough and solitary, but they're usually not suicidal."

"And not stupid," Meda said. "He could have held out in that station and yelled for help that would have wiped us and the car people out. This area is still patrolled."

Lorene got out of the car. Meda realized too late what she meant to do, reached out to stop her, but Lorene was too quick. She had shut the door and was exposed to the stranger. Eli and Meda moved in unspoken agreement to cover her. Later, if she survived, they could tell her what an ass she had been.

The man and anyone still inside the station could see both Lorene and her protectors. For the moment, this was another kind of stand-off.

"Can you believe she would risk her life for an ordinary little guy like that?" Meda asked.

Eli took a good look at the man. He was shorter than average, young—mid twenties, perhaps—overweight, though not grossly fat. His hair was a dull black with no hint of any other color even in the bright sunlight.

"She could have done worse," Eli said. "He hasn't got anything wrong with him. And that extra fat is a good thing, believe me." Her leaner brothers could have used it. "And for her, he's doubly attractive—uninfected and male. Hell, I hope she likes him once she has him."

Meda glanced at Eli. "She will. She won't be able to help herself."

"Is that so bad?" he asked.

She shrugged, said with bitter amusement, "How would I know? I'm as crazy as she is." She rested her hand on his shoulder, finally.

He kept the hand comfortably captive as he watched the man and Lorene. The man was clearly afraid—not of Lorene, but of the two rifle barrels he could see protruding from the Ford. But he was also determined. Either he would live or he would die, but he would not do any more hiding.

"She's got him," Meda said.

Eli had seen. Lorene, clearly unarmed, had offered to shake the man's hand. With a look of uncertainty and dawning relief, the man had given his hand, then jumped as she scratched him. He jerked his hand away, but let her catch it again as she apologized. To Meda's visible disgust, Lorene kissed the hand. Thin as she was now, Lorene was still pretty. The black-haired man was obviously impressed with her—and confused and still suspicious.

"I think it's okay," Eli said. "I'm going over there."

"She doesn't need your help," Meda protested.

He ignored her, got out of the car, opened her door, and waited for her to get out. "Come on," he said. "Seeing an old pregnant woman like you will help keep him calm. Maybe we won't have to hurt him."

For a moment, she looked as though she might punch him, but he grinned at her. She sighed and shook her head, then walked with him to Lorene and her stranger.

"It's okay," Lorene said. "His name is Andrew Zeriam. He was a prisoner. That Tien's his truck."

"Is it?" Eli wanted to see the man's face when he answered. He did not trust Lorene's quick acceptance. The organism and her glands were doing too much of her thinking for her just now. "The car family kept you alive?" he asked Zeriam.

The man stared at him hostilely. "They did," he said. "And the truck's mine." He looked ready to fight if he had to. Not eager, but ready. "They would have killed me soon," he said. "They were planning to."

He was soft and plump and young. One of the car people had probably taken a liking to him. They might not have killed him at all if he had cooperated. His voice, his face, his posture said he had not. He was not a homosexual, then—fortunately for Lorene. And if no one dug too deeply into what had been done to him during his captivity, Lorene might be able to convince him to come with her willingly.

"I'm going to get that sewage out of my truck and get out of here," he said suddenly.

"No!" Lorene said quickly.

Zeriam looked at her. There was no softness in his eyes. He looked from her to Eli, questioning.

Eli shrugged. "She likes you."

"Who are you people?"

"Not another car family, man, don't worry. Shit, we just pulled in here to pick up some auto supplies. Tried to get out when we saw what was going on, but those fools wouldn't let us."

"I saw. I hate to say it, but I'm glad they wouldn't. You probably saved my life." He hesitated. "Listen . . . can I help you fix that tire?"

"Thanks," Eli said. "What happened to the stationmaster?"

Zeriam turned away. "God, I managed to forget about her for a couple of minutes. One of the women from the car family decoyed her out. The car rat limped in all alone, pretended to be having car trouble. She had to go through a half hour of pretending to try to fix the car and crying and giving a performance that should have been on TV before the stationmaster would come out to help. This is strictly a self-service station, you know. Stick in your cash or card and push the button. But the stationmaster took pity, came out, and the gang came in and grabbed her. While they were busy with her, I made it into the station."

"Did they kill her?" Eli asked.

"No. They get more fun out of killing people slowly."

"You don't look like they've done much to you," Lorene said.

Zeriam turned without looking at her and walked away toward his truck.

"Look," Eli told Lorene, "you lay off that one subject and show him how much you like him and we won't have to use force. You'll have him willing now as well as later."

"But why—"

"Lori," Meda said with more understanding than Eli would have expected. "That's not asking much. Don't you want him enough to do that?"

Lorene wet her lips and went after Zeriam.

Meda came to stand beside Eli. "The guy's nothing to look at," she said, "but there may be more to him than I thought."

"Yeah."

"Want me to help change that tire?"

"Hell no. What do you want to do? Have the kid early? Why don't you go in the station and see what's there that we can use. Without the stationmaster, this place is finished, anyway."

"There should be a Highway Patrol copter out here sooner or later," she said. "The stationmaster probably had a check-in schedule with them that she won't be keeping now."

"So we'll hurry."

Still she hesitated. "Eli, what do you think of that guy, really?"

Eli shrugged. "I think he's okay. And I think he might not want to go home right now. I think he might start to see Lorene as just what he needs."

She nodded. "That was the impression I got." She went into the station, finally. That was when Zeriam came over without Lorene to talk to Eli.

"You know she's trying to get me to join you," he said bluntly.

"I know," Eli told him.

"What the hell would I be joining?"

Eli smiled. "A little nineteenth-century ranch in mountains you can't even see from here. Chickens, hogs, rabbits . . . The place will work your ass off. So will she, I expect."

The man did not smile. "How many others?"

"One other. A woman."

"Three women? How the hell did you wind up with three women?"

Eli's smile vanished. "Accidentally," he said. "The way you wound up here accidentally."

They stared at each other for several seconds, Zeriam clearly not liking Eli's evasion, but not quite as willing to probe it as he had been. "So you live on a ranch with your harem. What do you need me for?"

"Nothing," Eli said. He jerked a thumb toward Lorene who waited beside the Tien Shan. "She needs you."

"What about you?"

"I don't care. You're welcome as long as you'll share the work."

"What about Lorene?"

"What about her?"

Silence.

Eli gave a short laugh. "I don't own anybody, man. People do what they want to. If she likes you, she likes you."

Zeriam spent several seconds squinting at him in the sun. "Why do I believe you?" he said finally. "After that shit with the car gang, why should I believe anybody?"

"You dump your garbage?" Eli asked.

"The body? Yeah. Good shooting."

"Why don't you fuel up then. The ranch is a long way from here over a lot of lonely dirt roads."

They stared at each other for a moment longer, then Zeriam looked over at Lorene. She stood where she had been, waiting beside his truck, watching intently, and, though Zeriam did not realize it, listening.

Finally Zeriam went to her. She got into the truck with him and they drove around to the fuel lot.

PRESENT 18

Keira knew what she wanted.

She was afraid Eli would leave without giving it to her because she was young and ill. She was afraid touching would be enough for him. But he showed no signs of wanting to leave.

"Why?" he asked her, rubbing her bare arms beneath the caftan's loose sleeves. "I never tried so hard to spare someone. Why did you do it?"

She liked the way his hands felt. Not bruising or scratching. Just rubbing gently. If everything he'd told her was true, he was enjoying it more than she was. She closed her eyes for a moment, wondering whether he really wanted his question answered. She did not think he did.

"I didn't want to be alone," she said. That was true, as far as it went. "And you. Why didn't you aim that guy Kaneshiro at me when he asked about me?"

His expression hardened and his hands closed around her arms. She smiled. "I think I want to answer your question honestly," she said. "I think I can say it to you."

She hugged him, then backed away, escaping his hands. The hands twitched and he took a step toward her.

"Wait," she said. "Only for a moment. Bear it for a moment while I tell you."

He stood still.

She took a deep breath, met his eyes. "I think . . ." she began, "I *know* part of the reason I want you is that I'm . . . dying. But it is you I want. Not just a warm body. Before you I didn't want anyone. There were some guys who wanted me, even after I got sick, but I never . . . I thought I would never . . ." She floundered helplessly, unable to finish, wishing she had not begun. At least he did not laugh at her.

"You might die," he said. There was no conviction in his voice. "Stephen Kaneshiro needs a woman whose chances are better. And you . . . I wanted you with me."

She let out a breath she had not known she was holding and tried to go back to him.

"Wait a minute," he said, holding her at arm's length. "Maybe I have a couple of things to say to you, too. I want you to know me. God knows why. It's always been to my advantage not to have people know me that well at first."

"You know why," she said quietly.

He could not keep his hands off her so he settled for holding one of her hands.

"You have a son," she said. "Who's his mother?"

"Meda."

"Meda?"

"She and I have two sons."

"You're married then?"

He smiled. "Not formally. Besides, I have four more kids by other women."

She stared at him, first in surprise, then imagining what her mother would have said about him. "I've heard about . . . men who do that," she said.

He smiled grimly. "Your mama told you to keep the hell away from sewer rats like that, didn't she?"

"At least." She wondered why she did not pull her hand away from him. Six children by five different women. Good God. "Why?" she demanded.

"Young women survive," he said. "Right now, we have the best balance we've ever had between men and women. Kaneshiro is the only extra man we've ever had. Now he's not extra any longer."

"But I am."

"You and your father, because you're related."

"So when women are extra, you get them."

"That's exactly right. And when men are found for them, I give them up. We began that way out of biological necessity. I was alone with three women. The organism doesn't permit celibacy for any reason other than isolation."

"But . . . What about Meda?"

"What about her?"

"Why do you have two kids with her?"

"She's as close to a wife as I'm ever likely to get." He looked a little wistful. "We always get back together."

"But . . . right now, she's with my father."

"Yes."

"You don't care?"

"I care—though not as much as I would if she weren't already a couple of months pregnant. She's taking care of your father and I'm taking care of you."

And Rane was alone, Keira thought. At least Eli had said she was. Keira wondered why she tended to believe him so easily. She wondered why the things he was telling her were not more disturbing. He was everything her mother had warned her against and more. And she did not doubt that her mother had been right.

Yet all she regretted was that she would not be able to keep him. Her own feelings were so irrational, they frightened her.

"If I told you I didn't want to be part of your harem," she said, "would you go away?"

She felt the hand that held hers stiffen. "I don't think so," he said. "I don't think I could."

She thought if she were ever going to be afraid of him, now would be the time. "Let go of me," she whispered.

His grip on her tightened, became painful, then was suddenly released. His hands were shaking. He looked at them with amazement. "I didn't even think I could do that." He swallowed. "I can't keep doing it."

"That's okay," she said. She took his hand again and felt the shaking stop. He gave her a slow smile that she had not seen before. It confused her, warmed her. She gave him her other hand, but felt utterly foolish because she could no longer look directly at him.

Because he did nothing for a while, apparently felt no need to hurry, she regained her composure. "You like what you are, don't you," she said.

"I didn't care much for it today."

"Because of me." She managed to look at him again. "But you like what you are most of the time. You think you shouldn't like being a majority of one, but you do like it."

He held her by the shoulders. "Girl, if you convert okay and get even more perceptive, you're going to be spooky."

She laughed, then looked at his hands. "Don't you have to scratch me or something?"

"I would if I weren't so sure I didn't have to."

"What?"

He drew her to him, kissed her until she drifted from surprise at the thrust of his tongue to pleasure at the way he warmed her with his hands.

"You see," he said. "Who the hell needs biting and scratching?"

She laughed and let him lift her onto the bed.

She expected to be hurt. She had read enough and heard

enough not to expect the first time to be romantic and beautiful. And there was her illness to make things worse. She had never known it to make anything better. At least her medicine was still working.

Somehow, he managed not to hurt her much. He handled her like a fragile doll. She did not think she could have stood that from anyone else, but from him, it was a gift she readily accepted. She had some idea what it cost him.

Eventually, pleased and tired, they both slept.

It was ten to two when Keira awoke. She stumbled off to the bathroom, her mind barely awake until she saw the clock on the bookcase. Ten to two. Two. Oh God.

Eli himself had given her reason to go. If she stayed and somehow lived, he would pass her on to some other man. She did not want to be passed on.

And she did not want her father to leave without her—or try to leave and be killed because she could have helped and had not.

By the time she came out of the bathroom, she had made up her mind. But how to get away from Eli? The door was locked. She had no idea where the key was. In his clothing, perhaps.

But if she went searching through his clothing, then unlocking the door, he would awaken, stop her, and she would not get another chance.

She would have to hurt him.

She cringed from the thought. He had gone to some trouble to avoid hurting her. He was not exactly a good man, but she liked him, could have loved him, she thought, under other circumstances.

Yet for her father, she had to hurt him. After all, he had not only the key to the room door, but the keys to the Wagoneer. Without the car keys, her father might have to spend too much time getting into the car and getting it started. He would be caught before he drove a foot.

There was the clock—a nondigital antique with a luminous

dial. It ticked loudly and needed neither batteries nor electricity. If she hit Eli with it, he could probably be hurt, but would he be knocked unconscious or would he wake up and knock her unconscious? The clock was heavy, but awkward and big. The elephant bookend would be better. She had noticed it when she put away the book she had tried to read. The space between the elephant's trunk and its body offered a good handhold. The base was flat and would do less damage, less gouging and cutting when she hit him. It was unpainted cast iron, dull gray, heavy, and already just above Eli's head on the headboard bookshelf.

She went back to the bed, climbed in.

"Hey," Eli said sleepily. He reached for her. The gentleness of his hands told her he probably wanted to make love again. She would have given a great deal to stay there with him.

Instead, she reached for the elephant, gripped its trunk, and brought it down with all her strength on his head.

He gave a cry not much different from the one he had given at orgasm. Frightened, she hit him again. He went limp.

She had hurt her own hands and arms with the force of her blows. She knew she was weak, had feared at first that she could not really hurt him at all. Now she feared she had killed him.

She checked quickly to see that he was still breathing, still had a strong pulse. She found blood on his head, but not much of it. He was probably all right.

She got off the bed, pulled on her caftan, and stepped into her shoes, then she tore into his scattered clothing. She found the car keys at once, but could not find the one for the room. The door was definitely locked, though she could not remember him stopping to lock it. And there was no key.

She went to one of the larger of the four windows. It was not locked with a key, but it was closed so tightly she could not budge it. She could break it, of course, but that would bring any number of people running.

On the bed, Eli made a whining sound, and she tore at the window. It opened inward rather than upward, but it had apparently been painted shut.

She tried the other large window and found the same thing.

Finally she tried the two smaller center windows. When one of them opened, she dragged a chair to it, thankful for the rug that muffled the sound. She spent long desperate seconds trying to get the screen open.

In the end, she broke the catch, pushed the screen out, and jumped.

PART 4

REUN1ON

"I feel like hell," Andrew Zeriam whispered. "Everything stinks. Food tastes like shit. Light hurts my eyes . . ." He groaned.

"You want me to go away?" Eli asked. He spoke very softly. Zeriam sat in a darkened room—he had refused to lie down—and held his ears in this silent desert place, trying to shut out sounds he had not noticed before. What, Eli wondered, would happen if the disease spread to the cities? How would newly sensitive ears endure the assault of noise?

"Hell no, I don't want you to go away," Zeriam whispered. "I asked you to come in, didn't I?"

Silence.

"Can you see me, Eli? I can see you, and that's some trick."

"I can see you."

"It's pitch dark in here. It must be. It's night. The windows are shut. The lights are out. *It's dark!*"

"Yeah."

"Talk to me, Eli. Tell me what the hell is going on."

"You know what's going on. Lorene told you yesterday."

More silence. Then: "What are you that you can sit there and admit what she said is true?"

"I'm what you are, Andy—host to millions, or more likely billions, of extraterrestrials."

Zeriam lunged at him, swinging. Zeriam was faster and better coordinated then he had been, but he was not yet significantly stronger. Eli caught him, held him easily.

"Andy, if you don't sit your ass down or lie down, you're going to make me hurt you."

Zeriam stared at him, then burst into bitter laughter. "Hurt me? Man, you've killed me. You've killed . . . Shit, you may have killed everybody. Who knows how far this plague of yours will spread."

"I don't think I've killed you," Eli said. "I think you're going to live."

That stopped Zeriam's words and his struggles. "Live?"

"Your symptoms are like mine—weird, nerve-wracking, but not devastating. People who don't make it can't even stand up when they're as far along as you are. Hell, you're not even shaky."

"But . . . people die of this. Lorene's husband, Gwyn's . . ."

"Yeah. Some people do. The women didn't. I didn't. You probably won't."

"But you did this to me. You, ultimately, because you did it to Lorene. You're worse than a goddamn Typhoid Mary!"

"A what?" Eli asked. Zeriam had just become a history teacher a few months before his capture by the car family. Eli was used to either questioning or ignoring his historical allusions.

"A carrier," Zeriam said. "A disease carrier so irresponsible she had to be locked up to keep her from spreading her disease."

"It's not irresponsibility," Eli told him. "It's compulsion. You don't know anything about it yet—though you will. If I brought you an uninfected person now, you wouldn't be able to prevent yourself from infecting him. If you were without a mate the way Lorene was, nothing short of death could stop you from infecting a woman."

"I don't believe you!"

"You believe every word. You feel it. And you can't hide your feelings from us."

Zeriam turned away, paced across the room, then back. He glared at Eli. He looked around like a trapped animal.

"Andy?"

Zeriam did not answer.

"Andy, there's something you haven't noticed yet. Something that might help you realize you can have a life here."

"What?"

"Lorene is pregnant."

"She's what? Already? I've only been here three weeks."

"You two didn't waste any time."

"I don't believe you. You can't be sure."

"You're the one who can't be sure. I noticed the change because I've seen it before."

"What change in only three weeks?"

"She smells different," Eli said.

"You're crazy. She smells fine. She—"

"I didn't say she smells bad. Just different. It's a difference you'll learn to recognize."

"Hell, I ought to tell you how you smell."

"I know how I smell, Andy—especially to you. I've been through all this before. And you should keep in mind that you're beginning to smell as threatening, as wrong to me as I do to you. Later, we'll have to get used to each other all over again. The organism seems to pull women together and push men apart—at least at first." Eli sighed. "Now we can be men and work this out, work the ranch with the women and keep the disease to ourselves as much as possible, or we can let the organism make animals of us and we can kill each other—for nothing."

"We get a choice? It's not another compulsion?"

"No, just a strong inclination. But it will rule you if you let it. Lay back, and it will drive you like a car."

"So what are you doing? Holding it all at bay by sheer willpower? You're so full of shit, Eli!"

He was giving in to the organism, letting the smell of a "rival" male enrage him. No doubt it was easy. Anger was so much more satisfying than the uncertainty he had been feeling. He did not yet understand how easily his anger could get out of hand.

Eli stood up. "I'll send Lorene in," he said as he moved toward the door. Zeriam was bright. He would learn to handle inappropriate passions eventually. Meanwhile, Eli decided it was his responsibility to avoid dominance fights Zeriam could lose so easily and so finally.

Eli did not quite make it to the door. Zeriam grabbed his arm. "Why should you send her in here?" he demanded. "Keep her! You had her before. For all I know, it's your kid she's carrying!"

He was not saying what he believed. He had given himself over to the organism for the first time. There was no thought behind his words—nor behind his swing a moment later.

Eli caught his hand in mid-swing, held it, hit him open-handed before Zeriam could swing again. Eli struck twice more. He was in control because he knew Zeriam could not hurt him. If he had let the organism control him, if he had acted as though he were truly threatened, he would have killed Zeriam, and perhaps not even realized it until later, when he regained control.

As it was, Zeriam was not seriously hurt. He would have fallen, but Eli caught him and put him in a chair. There, he sat, nursing a split lip and coming out of a rage that had probably surprised even him.

"Eli," he said after a while, "how much of what you do is what you really want to do—or at least, what you've decided on your own to do." He paused. "How much of *you* is left?"

"You're asking how much of you will be left," Eli said.

"Yeah."

"A lot. Most of the time, a lot."

"And sometimes . . . insanity."

"Not insanity, Andy. Now is the most irrational time you'll have to face. Get through this, and you'll be able to deal with the rest."

Zeriam stared at him, then looked away. He was frightened, but he said nothing.

Later that night, he sat at the kitchen table and wrote Lorene a long, surprisingly loving letter. There was no bitterness in it, no anger. He wrote a longer letter to his unborn child. He had convinced himself it would be a son. He talked about the impossibility of spending his life as the carrier of a deadly disease. He talked about his fear of losing himself, becoming someone or something else. He talked about courage and cowardice and confusion. Finally, he put the letters aside and cheated the microbe of the final few days it needed to tighten its hold on him. He took one of Meda's sharp butcher knives and cut his throat.

PRESENT 20

Blake worried about having to use lights to stay on the poorly marked dirt trail. He had night glasses—glasses that utilized ambient light—but he was afraid to trust them in this dangerous, unfamiliar place. Yet he knew he was giving Eli's people a beacon to follow—and he had no doubt they were following.

"I saw something," Rane said, right on cue. She had climbed into the back because the seats in front were intended for only two. "Dad, they're coming. Three or four of them. You can see them when the mountains aren't directly behind them. They're running without lights."

"They can see in the dark," Keira said.

"So they say," Rane answered contemptuously. "Anyway, unless their cars are as different as they are, I don't see how they can catch us."

"Keep your head down," Blake told her. "They could have guns with night scopes. If they do, they can see in the dark all right. And they know these roads."

"Where will we go?" Keira asked.

Blake thought about that, glanced at his dashboard compass. They were heading due north. To reach the mountaintop ranch, they had traveled southeast, then south. "Kerry, take a look at the map," he said. "Use I-Forty as your northernmost point and the Colorado River bed as your easternmost. Give it fifty miles west of the river bed and south of the highway. Look for towns and a real road. We'll probably have to go all the way back to Needles, but at least there should be a road."

"I wouldn't be surprised," Keira said as she turned on the map and keyed in the area he had specified. He glanced over, saw Needles in the upper right hand corner of the screen and nodded.

"I didn't think any place could be as isolated as that ranch seemed to be," Keira said. "U.S. Ninety-five runs north to Needles. The problem is, I don't know where we are—how far we are from it. It might be to our advantage to stay on this road until we reach I-Forty."

Blake glanced at the map again. "Since we didn't cross Ninety-five on the way to the ranch, it has to be east of us."

Keira nodded. "Yes, maybe six or seven miles east, and maybe a lot more."

"Damn!" Blake grunted as the car bounced into and out of a hole. "I'm going to turn off as soon as I get the chance."

"We could wind up going twice as far as necessary," Rane said.

"Take another look behind you," Blake told her.

Both girls looked. Keira gasped when she saw how much closer the pursuers were.

"Watch for a turnoff," Blake said. "Any turnoff. I need a road I can see."

Keira leaned back in her seat, eyes closed. "Dad, Ninety-five has 'travel at your own risk' signs all over it."

He glanced at her. She knew what she was saying could not matter, but she had had to say it.

" 'High crime area,' " Rane read over Keira's shoulder. "It's a sewer! I didn't know they existed in the desert."

Blake said nothing. He had treated patients from city sewers —people so mutilated they no longer looked human, would never look human again in spite of twenty-first-century medicine. What the rat packs did to each other and to unprotected city-dwellers was not something he wanted to expose his daughters to. They knew about it, of course. The small armies of police who guarded enclaves kept out intruders, but they could not keep out information. Still, for sixteen years, he had managed to shield his daughters from the contents of sewers and cesspools. Now he was taking them into a sewer.

The turnoff they had been hoping for materialized suddenly out of the night, marked only by a dead Joshua tree. Blake turned. The new road was better—smooth, graded, straight. He increased his speed, slowly pulling away from the pursuers. The Wagoneer could travel. With it's modified engine it was much faster now than it had been when it was made—as long as it was not running a half-seen obstacle course.

Just over six miles later, the second dirt road ran into a paved highway—U.S. 95. They had gone from north to northeast. Now they were headed north again on a road that would take them to Needles—to safety.

Abruptly there were headlights directly in front of them— two cars coming toward them on the wrong side of the highway. Two cars that clearly did not intend to let him pass.

Reacting without thinking, Blake swung right. To his amazement, he discovered he was turning onto a road he had not noticed—another paved surface that headed him back almost in the direction from which he had come. Back toward the ranch.

He was being herded, Blake realized. They were on the eastern side, the wrong side of 95 now, but it had not taken much to force him to turn the first time. He could be turned again, made to recross the highway. All his effort so far could be for nothing.

How had Eli's people gotten ahead of him?

He switched out the lights and turned off the road onto a dry wash. At almost the same moment, Keira shut off the glowing screen of the map. Now, let Eli's people prove how well they could see in the dark. Nothing, *nothing* would force Blake back to the ranch—force him out of the profession of healing and into a life of spreading disease. *Nothing!*

Lights.

A dirt road, smooth and level, cut across the wash just ahead.

And along that road came a car. Only one. It could be a coincidence—some rancher going home, some hermit, a fragment of a car family, even lost tourists. But Blake was in no mood to take chances with anyone.

He turned onto the dirt road toward the oncoming car. Abruptly, he switched on his lights and accelerated.

The other car braked, skidded through the dust, swerved off the road into a thick, ancient creosote bush.

Blake sped on, knowing the dirt road must lead back to 95. He switched out his lights again, praying.

"That was a van," Rane said. "Eli's people have cars and trucks, but I didn't see any vans."

"You think they let us see everything?" Keira asked.

"I don't think that van was one of Eli's."

"I don't care whose it was," Blake said tightly. "I'm not stopping until I reach either a hospital or the police. We're not giving this damned disease to anyone else!"

"When Eli comes," Keira said softly, "it will be to kill us, recapture us, or die trying. He won't be frightened into a ditch by lights."

Blake glanced at her. He could hear certainty and fear in her voice. For once, he realized, he agreed with her. Eli and his people would do absolutely anything to prevent the destruction of their way of life. He could understand that. The life they had at their nearly self-sufficient desert enclave was better than what most people had these days. But there was the disease—no, call it what it was, the invasion. And that had to be stopped at any cost.

He remembered the thing running alongside his car on all fours. Running like an animal, a cat. Jacob. It was possible if this insanity spread, *it was possible* that he could have grandchildren who looked like Jacob. Things. Christ!

The highway was ahead, down a slope. It looked empty and safe. Blake felt if he could reach it, he would have a chance.

He accelerated, swung onto the highway, headed north again.

"We've made it!" Rane shouted.

Keira looked around. "Someone's back there. I can see them."

"Sewage. I don't see any—"

Lights again. Lights behind them, then abruptly, lights in front.

Blake was not aware of making the choice not to slow down. Apparently that choice had been made before, once and for all. He thought he saw a human shape leap from one of the cars, but the car kept coming. At the last instant, Blake tried to swerve up the slope and around. He did not quite make it. The front left corner of the Wagoneer hit the other car and Blake's head hit the steering wheel.

There was nothing else.

PAST 21

Zeriam made it.

He almost failed, almost survived. He had done a thorough job on his neck, but it was half-healed when Meda found him dead. The front of his throat was gaping, but the sides were merely bloody and scarred.

Meda brought Eli to him. When Eli was able to think past shock, past sadness, past the terrible knowledge that Zeriam would eventually have to be replaced, he examined the man's neck.

"I wouldn't have made it," he said.

"Made what?" Meda asked.

"I wouldn't have died—even if I had managed to cut my throat. I'd heal all the way."

"From a cut throat without a doctor? I don't believe you."

"I was in a couple of dominance fights aboard ship." He paused, remembering, shuddered inwardly. "The first time, I was stabbed through the heart twice. I healed. The second time, I was beaten literally to a pulp with a chunk of metal. I healed. Barely a scar. It takes a lot to kill us."

She helped him clean up the blood. It was she who found the letters. They were sealed in envelopes and marked *"To Lorene"* and *"To my son."*

Meda stared at them for several seconds, then looked toward the bedrooms. "I'm going to wake Lorene," she said.

He caught her shoulder. "I'll do it."

She looked down and away from Zeriam. He felt her tremble and knew she was crying. She never liked him to see her when she cried. She thought it made her look ugly and weak. He thought it made her look humanly vulnerable. She reminded him that they were still humanly vulnerable in some ways.

For once, she let him hold her, comfort her. He took her out of the kitchen, back to their room and stayed with her for a few minutes.

"Go," she said finally. "Talk to Lorene. God, how is she going to stand this a second time?"

He did not know, did not really want to find out, but he got up to go.

"Eli?"

He looked back at her, almost went back to her; she looked so uncharacteristically childlike, so frightened. He did not understand why she was afraid.

"No, go," she said. "But . . . take care of yourself. I mean . . . no matter how strong you think this thing has made you, no matter what's happened to you . . . before, don't do anything careless or dumb. Don't . . ."

Don't die, she meant. She rubbed her stomach, looked at him. *Don't die.*

PRESENT 22

Blake regained consciousness in darkness.

He lay still, realizing that he was no longer in his car. He was lying on something flat and hard—a carpeted floor, he thought after a moment. His head ached—seemed to pulsate with pain. And he was cold.

His discomfort kept him from realizing immediately that his hands and feet were bound. Even when he tried to rub his head and discovered he had to move both arms, he did not understand why at once. He thought there was something more wrong with his body. When, finally, he understood, he struggled, tried to free himself, tried to stand up. He managed only to writhe around and sit up.

"Is anyone here?" he said.

There was no answer.

He squinted, trying to penetrate the darkness, fearing that he might be blind. He remembered hitting his head as he sheared into the oncoming car. He probably had a concussion. And what else?

Finally, dizzily, he managed to turn around, see dim light outlining draperies. He could still see, then.

"Thank God," he muttered.

"Dad?"

He started. "Rane?" he said. "Is that you?"

"It's me." She sounded half awake. "Are you okay?"

"Fine," he lied. "Where the hell are we?"

"A ranch house. Another ranch house."

"Another . . . ?"

"It wasn't Eli's people, Dad. I mean, they were chasing us, too, but they didn't catch us. A car gang caught us."

That took a moment to sink in. "Oh God."

"They think they can get a ransom for us. I made them look at your identification. Meanwhile, they've been exposed to the disease."

"If there was no break in their skins—"

"There was. I scratched one myself. He tore my shirt open and I tore some skin off his arm."

That shook Blake from one kind of misery to another. "Are you all right?"

"Yeah. A few bruises, that's all. Before anyone could rape me, they decided I might be worth more . . . intact."

"And Keira?"

"They let her alone too. She's right here. She was awake for a while—said she felt awful. Said she'd left all her medicine at Eli's."

"Is she tied?"

"We both are."

He tried to see them, thought he could see Rane sitting up. "Shall I wake Keira?"

"Let her sleep. That's the only medicine she has left now. How long was I unconscious?"

"Since last night. But you weren't always unconscious. Every now and then you'd mumble and move around. And you threw up. They made me clean it with my hands still tied."

Concussion. And he had lost a day. He had also lost his freedom again. Worst of all, he had spread the disease. He had failed at all he had attempted. All. . . .

"There's going to be an epidemic," Rane whispered.

Blake inched over toward her, groped for her.

"What are you doing?"

"Give me your hands."

"Dad, we're not tied with ropes. That's probably why I can still feel my hands and feet. We're wearing cuffs—choke-cuffs."

Blake lay down again heavily. "Shit," he muttered. Everything the car family did to hold them sealed its doom and increased the likelihood of an epidemic. He tested the cuffs, doing what he could first to slip them, then to pull their bands apart. They were plastic, but felt surprisingly soft and comfortable as long as he did not try to get rid of them. Once he began to struggle, however, they tightened until he thought they would cut off his hands.

Pain stopped him. And the moment he relaxed, the cuffs eased their grip. People could be left hobbled as he was indefinitely. Choke-cuffs were called humane restraints. Blake had heard that in prisons—inevitably overcrowded—order was sometimes maintained by the threat of hobbling with such humane restraints. Hobbled prisoners were not isolated. They were left in with the general prison population—fair game. They frequently did not survive.

Lying on his back, helpless, eaten alive with frustration and fear, Blake knew how they must have felt.

Would it be possible to talk to the car family? Would there be even one member intelligent enough to understand the danger? And if there were one, what evidence could Blake show him? The bag was gone. Neither he nor the girls had symptoms yet. If Meda was right, there would be symptoms in a few days, but how far could a car family spread the disease in a few days?

"Is this their base?" he asked Rane. A true car family had no base, he knew, except their vehicles.

"This place isn't theirs," Rane said. "They took it. They killed the men and raped the women. I think they're still keeping some of the women alive somewhere else in the house."

Blake shook his head. "God, this is a sewer. There's only one source of help that I can think of—and I don't want to think of it."

"What? Who?"

"Eli."

"Dad . . . Oh no. His kind . . . they aren't people anymore."

"Neither are these, honey."

"But, please, I gave these all the information they needed to convince Grandmother and Granddad Maslin that we're prisoners. They'll ransom us."

"What makes you think people as degenerate as these will let us go after they get what they want?"

"But they said . . . I mean, they haven't hurt us." She groped for reassurance. "Let's face it. Grandmother and Granddad would ransom us if we were alive at all—no matter what had been done to us, but the car people haven't done anything."

Blake sat up, tried to see her in the darkness. "Rane, don't say that again. Not to anyone." If only she thought before she opened her mouth. If only she hadn't opened her mouth at all. *If only no other listener had heard!*

Unexpectedly, Keira spoke into the silence. "Dad? Are you there?"

Blake shifted from anger at Rane to concern for Keira. "We're both here. How do you feel?"

"Okay. No, lousy, really, but it doesn't matter. We were worried about you. You took so long to regain consciousness. But now that you're awake, and it's night . . . what would you think about one of us hopping over to one of those windows and signaling Eli's people?"

Silence.

"Rane wouldn't let me do it," Keira added.

Blake touched Rane. "So you had thought of it."

"Not me. I would never have thought of that. Keira did. Dad, please. Eli's people . . . I couldn't stand to go back to them. I'd rather stay here."

"Why?" Blake asked. He thought he knew the answer, and he did not really want to hear her say it, but it needed to be said. She surprised him.

"I can't stand them," she said. "They're not human. Their children don't even look human. . . . Yet they're seductive. They could have pulled me in. That guy, Kaneshiro . . ."

"Did he hurt you?"

"You mean did he rape me? No! There'd be nothing seductive in that. Nobody raped me. But in a little while, a few days, he wouldn't have had to. I'm afraid of those people. I'm scared shitless of them."

"That's the way I feel about these car people!" Keira said. "Rane . . . so what if you were sort of . . . seduced by Eli's people. I was, too. All it meant to me was that they weren't really bad people—not the way rat packs are bad. They're different and dangerous, but I'd rather be with them than here."

Blake began to inch across the room, making as little noise as possible. Hopping would have been too noisy.

"Dad, don't!" Rane begged.

He ignored her. If any of Eli's people were outside, he wanted them to know where he was. It was possible, of course, that they would simply shoot him, but he did not believe they would—they could have done that long ago. The *Clay's Ark* people wanted their captives—their converts—back. Perhaps by now they also wanted any salvageable members of the car gang and the ranch family. Mainly, they wanted to keep the disease from spreading, keep it from destroying their way of life. They had been totally unrealistic to think they could go on hiding indefinitely, but at the moment Blake was on their side.

He reached the window, managed to stand up, almost pulling down the drapes in the process. The leg restraints tightened as he stood.

The moon was waning, but still bright in the clear desert air. It was possible that someone outside might be able to see him in the moon and starlight, but he hoped Eli's people had told the truth when they claimed to be able to see in the dark. He pushed the draperies to one side and stood in plain view of anything outside. He could see hills not far distant. Before them was a shadowy jumble of huge rocks—as though there had been a slide —or perhaps merely weathering away of soil. The rocks could provide excellent cover for anyone out there.

Off to one side was a building that might have been a barn. From the barn extended a corral. The barn looked spare and modern. The people of this ranch had not lived in the nineteenth century. It was possible that even the cuffs had been theirs. A car family would not care whether restraints were humane or not.

Scanning as carefully as he could, Blake could see no sign of anyone. Still, he stood there, at one point holding up his hands to show that they were bound. He felt foolish, but he did not sit down until he felt he had given even an intermittent watcher a chance to see him.

Finally, he hopped away from the window and let himself down quietly so that he could roll back to where the girls were. He had not quite made it when the door opened and someone switched on a light. He found himself squinting upward into the face of a squat, burly man in an ill-fitting, new shirt and pants that were almost rags.

"Looks like you're going to live," he said to Blake.

Blake rolled onto his back and sat up. "I'd say so."

"Your people want you. Big surprise."

"I'm sure most of your victims have people who want them."

The man frowned at Blake as though he thought Blake might be making fun of him. Then he gave a loud, braying laugh. "Most of you walled-in types don't give a piss for each other, Doc. You don't know family like we do. But the hell with that. What I want to know is who else wants you?"

Blake sat up straighter, staring at the man. "What do you mean?"

The man pushed Blake over gently with his foot. "Those your own teeth, Doc?"

Blake writhed back into a sitting position. "Look, I'll tell you what I know. I just wanted to find out what's happened since I've been unconscious."

"Nothing. Now who else wants you?"

Blake wove a fantasy about Eli's people, made them just another rat pack with ideas no loftier than this one's. Ransom. He said nothing about the disease. There was nothing he could say to a man like this, he realized. Nothing that would not get his teeth kicked in. Or if the man believed him, he might shoot Blake and both girls, then run—on the theory that if he got away fast enough, he could escape the disease. Blake had known men like him before; confronting them with unfamiliar ideas was dangerous even in controlled, hospital surroundings.

He got absolutely no response from the man until he mentioned the mountaintop ranch. The moment he said it, he knew he was talking too much.

"Those people!" the burly man muttered. "I been planning for a long time to bury them. Maybe not bother to kill them first. Bony, stripped-down models. Shit, you're a doctor. What's the matter with those guys?"

"They never gave me a chance to find out," Blake lied. "I think they're taking something." Drugs. That was something a sewer rat could understand.

"I *know* they're taking something," the man said. "One time I saw a couple of them running down jack rabbits and eating them. I mean like a coyote or a bobcat, tearing into them before they were all the way dead."

Blake blinked, repelled and amazed. "You *saw* them do *that?*"

"I said I did, didn't I? What have they got, Doc, and what do you think it's worth?"

"I tell you, I don't know. We were prisoners. They didn't tell us anything."

"You got eyes. What did you see?"

"Dangerous, bone-thin people, faster than average, stronger than average, and close."

"What close?"

"They give a piss for each other. Listen, who are you, anyway?"

"Badger. I head this family."

He looked the part. "Well, Badger, I didn't get the impression these people knew how to forgive or forget. They probably see us as their property. They probably want us back—or maybe they'll settle for a share of our ransom."

"Share? You've got too much sun, man. Or they have. What are they doing, growing something?"

"I don't know!"

"I gotta know. I gotta find out! Shit, it must be good stuff."

"They look like a strong wind would blow them away, and you think they have good stuff?"

Badger kicked Blake again, this time less gently. Blake fell over. "You're a doctor," Badger said. "You ought to know! What the hell is it?" Another hard kick.

Through a haze of pain, Blake heard one of the girls scream, heard Badger say, "Get away from me, cunt!" heard a slap, another scream.

"Listen!" Blake gasped, sitting up. "Listen, they have a garden!" His head and his side throbbed. What if his ribs were broken? Meda had said broken bones would be fatal to him now. "Those people have a big garden," he said. "They never really let us see what they grew there. Maybe if you could—"

He was cut off by the crack of a shot. The sound echoed several times into a world that had otherwise gone silent. Another shot. It hit the window near them, somewhere near ceiling level, then ricocheted with an odd whine. More bulletproof glass. A house located where this one was was probably hardened as much as possible against any form of attack.

Someone outside had perhaps seen or heard Blake. Someone outside was either a bad shot trying to kill him or a good shot trying to protect him.

"Shit!" Badger muttered. He turned and ran from the room, slamming the door behind him.

"If we could break the windows," Keira said when he was gone, "Eli's people might come in and get us."

And Rane: "If bullets couldn't break them, we sure can't with our bare hands."

"But we've got to get out! That guy Badger is crazy. If he kicks Dad's ribs in, Dad will die!"

Blake lay listening to them, thinking he should say something reassuring, but now that the danger was less immediate, he could not make the effort. His side and head were competing with each other to see which could hurt more. He lay still, eyes closed, trying to breathe shallowly. He was desperately afraid one or more ribs were already broken, but he could do nothing. He felt consciousness slipping away again.

"I'm going to try something," he heard Keira say.

"There's nothing to try," Rane told her.

"Shut up. Let me do something for a change." She paused, then spoke in an ordinary voice. "Eli or whoever's out there, if you can hear me, fire three more times."

There was nothing.

"What did you expect?" Rane demanded. "All that stupid talk about seeing in the dark and being able to hear better than other people—"

"Will you shut up!" Keira tried again. "Eli," she said, "maybe we can distract them. We can help you get them. You'll want them now that they've been exposed to the disease. Help us and we can help you."

More silence.

Keira spoke again softly. "I'm sorry I had to hit you." She hesitated. "But I did have to. You told me I couldn't have you, then you made me choose between the little I could have and my father and sister. What would you have done?"

For a long while, there was no sound at all. Then it seemed to Blake in his pain, in his confusion at what he had heard his daughter say, he heard three evenly timed shots.

PART 5

JACOB

Meda wanted a girl.

Eli merely wanted Meda to survive and be well. When that was certain, he would concern himself with the child.

He worried about her in spite of his confidence in the organism's ability to keep its hosts alive. This was something new, after all. None of the *Ark*'s crew had been able to have children during the mission. Their anticonception implants had been timed to protect them and had worked in spite of the organism since no doctor had survived to remove them.

Before the *Ark* left, there had been discussion of the unlikely possibility (emphasized by the media and de-emphasized by everyone connected with the program) that the crew might find itself stranded and playing Adams and Eves on some alien world. Thus, the effectiveness of the implants was intended to last only through the time allotted to the mission and the quarantine period scheduled to follow it. In spite of everything, Eli had been pleased to discover that his had worn off right on time.

Another fear played up by the media and down by everyone in the program was the possibility that faster-than-light travel might have some negative effect on conception, pregnancy, and childbirth. The Dana Drive that powered the *Ark* involved an exotic combination of particle physics and psionics. Parapsychological mumbo jumbo, it had been called when Clay Dana presented it. Even when he was able to prove everything he said, even when others were able to duplicate his work and his results, there were outspoken skeptics. After years of tedious, uncertain observation of so-called psychic phenomena, after years of trickery by "psychic" charlatans, some scientists in particular found their prejudices too strong to overcome.

But the majority were more flexible. They accepted Dana's work as proof of the psionic potential—specifically, the psychokinetic potential—of just about everyone. Some saw this potential in military terms—the beginnings of a weapons delivery system as close to teleportation as humanity was likely to come. Others, including Clay Dana himself, saw it as a way to the stars. Clay Dana and his supporters demanded the stars. They had clearly feared turn-of-the-century irrationality—religious overzealousness on one side, destructive hedonism on the other, with both heated by ideological intolerance and corporate greed. The Dana faction feared humanity would extinguish itself on Earth, the only world in the solar system that could support human life. There were always hints that the Dana people knew more than they were saying about this possibility. But what they said in Congress, in the White House, to the people by way of the media, turned out to be enough—to the amazement of their opposition. The Dana faction won. The *Ark* program was begun. The first true astronauts—star voyagers—began their training.

Because of the psychokinetic element, a human crew was essential. The Dana drive amplified and directed human psychokinetic ability. Surprisingly, some people had too much psychokinetic potential. These could not be trusted with the drive. They over-controlled it, affected it when they did not intend to, made prototypes of the *Clay's Ark* "dance" off course. Only strange, old Clay Dana tested out as having too much ability, yet was able to control his drive with a psionic feather touch. Both Eli and Disa had been able to pilot the prototypes and later the *Ark* itself. This meant they were psionically ordinary. And for some reason, old Dana had taken a liking to them, though Disa admitted to being a little afraid of him. And what she felt about Dana, was what a lot of people watching their TV walls felt about the *Ark* crew and backup crew. People were curious, but a little afraid—and envious. Earth was becoming less and less a comfortable place to live. Thus it was necessary that the crew have weaknesses and face serious dangers. People knew children had been born on the moon and in space safely, but the gossip networks with their videophone-in shows and their instant polls, their inter-

views and popular education classes, jacked up their ratings with
hours of discussion of whether or not faster-than-light travel could
be dangerous to pregnant women and their children. There was
even a retrogressive women's protection movement intended to
keep women off the *Ark*.

Eli and Disa were too busy to pay much attention to TV
nonsense, as they thought of it, but they went along when the
implants were proposed. And Eli left frozen sperm behind—just
in case—and Disa left several mature eggs.

Now, Eli wished somehow that his frozen sperm could have
been used to impregnate Meda. He knew this was not a reasonable wish, under the circumstances, but he was not feeling very
reasonable. He watched Lorene walk Meda back and forth across
the room. Meda did not want to walk, but she had tried both
sitting and lying down. These, she said, made her feel worse.
Lorene walked her slowly, said it would not do her any harm.
Lorene had had some nursing experience at a birth center before
she married. She had trained to be a midwife to women too poor
to go to the better hospitals and too frightened to go to the others.

Meda stopped for a moment beside Eli's chair, rested her
hand heavily on his shoulder. "What are you doing?" she asked.
"Feeling guilty and helpless?"

He only looked at her.

She patted his shoulder. "Men are supposed to feel that way.
They do in the books I've read."

He could not help himself. He laughed, stood up, kissed her
wet forehead, then walked with her a little until she wanted to
sit down in the big armchair. He was surprised she did not want
to lie down, but Lorene did not seem surprised so he said nothing.
He pulled another chair over and sat beside her, holding her hand
and listening as she panted and sometimes made low noises in her
throat as the contractions came and went. He was terrified for her,
but he sat still, trying to show strength and steadiness. She was
doing all the work, after all, pushing, enduring the pain and risk,
giving birth to their child without the medical help she might
need. If she could do that and hold together, he could hold
together, too.

She never screamed or used any of the profanity she had picked up from him. In fact, she seemed surprised that the birth happened so easily. The baby, when it came, looked like a gray, hairless monkey, Eli thought. By the time Lorene had tied and cut the cord and cleaned the baby up, it was not gray any longer, but a healthy brown. Lorene wrapped it in a blanket and handed it to Meda, still in her chair. Meda examined it minutely, touching and looking, crying a little and smiling. Finally, she handed the child to Eli. He took it eagerly, needing to hold it and look at it and understand that this was his son.

The baby never cried, but it was clearly breathing well. Its eyes were calm and surprisingly lively. Its arms were long and slender—without the baby pudgyness Eli had expected, but he had no real idea how a newborn should look. Maybe they grew pudgy later, or maybe *Clay's Ark* babies never grew pudgy. It was enough that this baby seemed healthy and alert. Its legs were doubled against its body, but freed of the blanket, they straightened a little and kicked in the air. They were as long and slender as the arms. And the feet were long and narrow. Eli looked at the little face and the child seemed to look back curiously. He wondered how much it could see. It had a full head of thick, curly black hair and large ears. When it yawned, Eli saw that it already had several teeth. That could make nursing hard on Meda.

Eli reached for a tiny, thin hand and the boy grasped his finger surprisingly tightly. After a moment, Eli grinned.

The child startled him by smiling back at him. Somehow, it did not seem to be mirroring his grin. Its smile seemed almost sly —the unbabylike gesture of one who knew something he was not telling.

PRESENT 24

Somehow, Blake lost track of time. He was aware of sporadic shooting, aware that the house was under siege, that Rane and Keira were first with him, then gone. He worried about them when he realized they were gone, wondered where they were. He worried about his own helplessness and confusion.

Once the man called Badger came in to see him, bringing several other people along. The group shouted and stank and made Blake feel sicker than ever—all but one woman. She was no cleaner than the others, but her scent was different, compelling. She was just another car rat, but he found himself reaching out to her, groping for her with his cuffed hands. He heard shouts of laughter, then her voice, low and mocking.

"Hey there," she said, taking his hands. "You're not going to die on us, are you? Nobody'll buy you back dead." She had a deep, throaty voice that would have been sexy had it not been so empty of caring. He knew she was laughing at him—at his pain, at his helplessness, even at his interest in her. He knew, but all he could think about was that he wanted her. He could not help himself. Her scent drew him irresistibly. He tried to pull her down beside him. She laughed and pulled away.

"Maybe later, wallie," she whispered. At least she had the

kindness to whisper, not shout like the others. He was confused for a moment by her calling him "wallie." She knew his name. They all did. Then, murkily, he realized she was referring to the fact that he lived in a walled enclave. He wondered whether he would ever see it again.

The woman nudged him with her foot. "How about that?" she said. "Want me to come back when you're feeling better?"

Her friends brayed out their laughter.

But she did come back that night. And this time she only pretended to mock him as she unbound his hands and feet. "Don't do anything dumb now. You hurt me or get outside this room, Badger will cut your head off."

He opened his eyes and saw that she was nude, kneeling down beside him on the rug of his bare room. She fumbled with his belt. "Let's see what you've got, wallie. Big old rifle or little handgun."

For a moment, he thought she was Meda, but her hair, now free of the scarf she had worn before, was a startling white. She was a tall, sun-browned woman, plump, but not really fat. Her scent was incredible. It so controlled him, he could not focus on whether she was pretty or not. It did not matter.

He could not have thought he had the strength to hold her as he did with his newly freed hands and make love to her once and again and again. In the end, the woman seemed surprised herself, and pleased, willing to drop some of her car-rat emotional armor. Without being asked, she got him a blanket from somewhere. He remembered Rane and Keira trying to beg one for him, and being refused. They had tried to get extra food for him, too, and failed. When he asked the woman for food, she brought him a cold beer and a plate of bread and roast beef left over from the car gang's dinner. The gang, sealed in as it was, had been living off the ranch family's large pantry and freezer.

The meat was too well-done and too highly seasoned for Blake's newly sensitive taste, but he ate it anyway. The gang fed him as well as they ate themselves, but it was not enough. It was never enough. He consumed the extra meal ravenously.

"You eat like a damn coyote," the woman complained. "You want some more?"

He nodded, his mouth full.

She got him more and watched while he ate. He wondered why she stayed, but he did not mind. He did not want to be alone. The food made him feel much better—less totally focused on his discomfort. "Who the hell are you, anyway?" he asked.

"Smoke," she said, touching her hair.

"Smoke," he muttered. "First Badger, now Smoke."

"Those are our family names," she said. "We don't keep the same names once we're adopted into a family. My name before was Petra."

He smiled. "I like that better. Thank you, Petra."

To his surprise, she blushed.

"Are my daughters all right?" he asked

She looked surprised. "They're okay. They say you screamed at them to get out. Hell, we heard you screaming. And with what you were calling them, we didn't figure they were your blood daughters. We thought you might hurt them."

Screaming? He did not remember. Screaming at Rane and Keira? Why?

Fragments of what seemed to be a dream began to drift back to him. But it was a dream of Jorah, his wife, not of the girls. Jorah, smooth and dark as bittersweet chocolate, soft and gentle, or so people thought when they saw her or heard her voice. Later they discovered the steel the softness disguised.

The dream recaptured him slowly, and he could see her as she had been with the cesspool kids she taught. The kids liked her or at least respected her. They knew she cared about them. The bigger, more troublesome ones knew she had a gun. She was too idealistic for her own good, but she was not suicidal.

He saw her as she had been when he met her at UCLA. He was going to fight diseases of the body and she, diseases of a society that seemed to her too shortsighted and indifferent to survive. She preached at him about old-fashioned, long-lost causes —human rights, the elderly, the ecology, throwaway children, corporate government, the vast rich-poor gap and the shrinking middle class. . . . She should have been born twenty or thirty years earlier. He could not get particularly involved in her causes. He did not believe there was anything he could do to keep the country, the world from flushing itself down the toilet. He meant to take care of his own and do what he could for the others, but he had few illusions.

Still, he could not keep away from her. She was an earlier, happier compulsion. He let her preach at him because he was afraid if he did not, she would find someone else with open ears. He knew her family did not like her interest in him. They were people who had worked themselves out of one of the worst cesspools in the southland. They had nurtured Jorah's social conscience too long to let it fall victim to a white man who had never suffered a day in his life and who thought social causes were passé.

He married her anyway, had two daughters with her, even acquired something of a social conscience through her. Eventually, he began putting in time at one of the cesspool hospitals. It was like trying to empty the Pacific with a spoon, but he kept at it—as she kept at her teaching until a young sewer slug blew away most of the back of her head with a new submachine gun. The slug was thirteen years old. He did not know Jorah. He had just stolen the gun and wanted to try it out. Jorah was handy.

Why had Blake dreamed of her, then recalled her so vividly? And what did she have to do with his driving Rane and Keira away?

"Are they really your kids?"

He jumped, looked around, was surprised to see that Petra was still there.

"The two girls. Are they your kids?"

"Of course."

"Shit, I felt sorry for them. You were calling them sluts and whores and slugs and sewage—everything you could think of. One of them was crying."

"But . . . why would I do that?"

"You asking me? Hell, who knows? You hit your head pretty hard against the steering wheel. Maybe you just went crazy for a while."

"But . . ." But why had he dreamed of Jorah? Such a realistic dream—as though she were with him again. As though the utterly senseless killing had never happened. As though he could touch her, love her again.

Keira.

His mind flinched away from thinking of her. She was a too-thin, too-frail, younger version of Jorah. She had that same incredible skin. And she had, Blake knew, more of her mother's steel than most people realized.

Christ, had he tried to rape Keira?

Had he?

The girl was so weak. Could he have tried and failed? "Jesus," he whispered.

"You okay?" Petra asked.

He looked at her, realized she was only a few years older than Rane and Keira. A young girl, still able to drop the car-rat identity and take pleasure in doing so.

"I'm all right," he lied. "Listen, now that you've told me about the girls, I have to see them. One of them, at least. I have to apologize."

She looked away. "I don't know if I can bring them."

He understood her, and wished he had not. The girls might not be alone. "Try," he said, "please."

"Okay." But she stopped to kiss him and he was caught up again in the scent and feel of her. She giggled like a delighted child and lay down with him again.

By the time she went away and came back with Keira, he was badly frightened. He was no longer in control of himself. Tiny microbes controlled him, had forced him to have sex with a young girl when an instant before, sex had been the farthest thing from his mind. What had they made him do to his daughter?

Keira came into the room much as she had come into another room—how many days ago? Eli had released her then for a few painful minutes. Who had released her this time? God, what would Jorah think of the way he was taking care of their children?

"Dad?"

She had a bruise on the side of her face. It was swollen and puffy. She could not conceal the fact that she did not want to get near him. And, heaven help him, her scent was as good as Petra's had been.

"Did I hit you?" he asked, looking at her swollen face.

She shook her head. "Rane did."

"Why?"

She stared at him for several seconds. "You don't remember, do you?" She took a step farther back from him. "Jesus, I wish I didn't."

He said nothing, could not make himself speak.

She went to the window, pushed the drape aside, and seemed to examine the frame. "This house won't burn," she said. "Light it and it will smolder a little, then go out. Eli's people have tried lighting it a few times. I think one of them was shot in the attempt."

"They tried to burn the house with us in it?"

"Badger called for help on his radio. They heard him. Or if they didn't hear him, they heard me when I repeated what he said next to the kitchen window." She turned to face him. "I can hear them sometimes, Dad. When the car people aren't making too much noise, I can hear them talking. I heard Eli."

"Saying what?"

"That if everything goes okay, the car people will go over to him when their symptoms begin. If it doesn't, if the help Badger called for actually comes, Eli might have to sacrifice us."

"Sacrifice . . . ?"

"They have some explosives already planted. They don't want to do it, but . . . well, they can't let anyone in the house leave."

"Kerry, did I rape you?" He had said the words. And somehow, they had not choked him.

She swallowed, went to the door and stood beside it. "Almost."

"Oh God. Oh God, I'm sorry."

"I know."

"Rane stopped me?"

"Yes." She hesitated. "Rane stopped us. I . . . I wasn't exactly fighting."

He frowned, repelled and uncomprehending.

"Don't look at me like that," Keira said. "I know how I smell to you—and how you smell to me. I had to see you to be sure you were okay. But . . . I'm afraid of you—and of myself. It's so crazy.

Rane hit me mostly to get my attention so I'd stop fighting her when she tried to pull me away. She said when she hit you, you didn't seem to feel it." Keira rubbed her face. "I sure felt it."

Blake moved away from her because he wanted to move toward her so badly. "Were you hurt otherwise?"

"No."

"How do you feel?"

She stared past him, surprising him with the beginnings of a smile. "Hungry," she said. "Hungry again."

Keira believed she was going to live. She felt stronger and hungry. Her hearing was startlingly keen. That was enough for her. The fact that she was still a captive, still the carrier of a dangerous disease, still caught between warring gangs had almost ceased to matter to her. Those things could not cease to matter to Blake.

When Petra had taken Keira away, he went over the bare room as he could not have with bound hands and feet. He peeled back the rug, looking for loose flooring. He examined the walls, even the ceiling. Finally, he examined the closetlike bathroom— a toilet, a sink, and a tiny window that did not open. None of the windows opened. The air conditioning was good. The air stayed fresh and probably would until Eli decided to foul it, but the air-conditioning ducts were too small to be of use to Blake.

Because he was desperate, Blake tried pushing at the glass —or the plastic—in the window. It was only one small pane. It might be breakable.

It did not break. But the frame gave a little. Blake took off his shirt, wrapped his right hand in it, and as quietly as he could, began trying to pound the entire window out. Even if he knocked it loose, the hole would be almost too small to crawl through. But he felt stronger now, and anything would be better than sitting around like a caged animal, waiting for someone else to decide his fate.

When his right hand tired, he continued the pounding with

his left. The muffled sound was loud to him, but no one else seemed to notice. He realized now that he could not trust his hearing to tell him what sounds might be reaching normal people.

Finally, the window fell out onto the ground. The noise that it made when it hit and bumped against the house was loud. Blake heard someone call out, then heard the sound of approaching motors. Frightened, he hesitated. Keira had said Badger had called for reinforcements. What if he escaped from one group into the hands of another? On the other hand, if he stayed where he was, the window would be discovered and he would be shackled again. They would take no more chances with him.

As the sounds of approaching motors grew louder, he made up his mind. He was at the rear of the house. He could not see the road or the approaching cars or cycles so he was certain the newcomers would not be able to see him. Eli's people might see him, but he did not think they would shoot. He hoped he could escape them too and get real help. Medical help, finally. Meanwhile, he prayed they would rescue the girls and keep them safe —since he could no longer trust himself near them.

He feared that if he reached a town, a hospital, his chances of seeing the girls again would be slim. They would be going into Eli's world, going underground, becoming whatever the organism would make of them. He would be beginning a war against the organism.

He managed to squeeze out of the window, leaving a little skin behind, and drop quietly to the ground. He ran toward the rocks, expecting at every moment to be shot in the back or accosted from the rocks by Eli's people. But in front of the house, the approaching cars had arrived and the shooting had begun. All the hostilities were there.

Blake ran on. From the rocks, he could climb into the hills and get a look around. He could find out where the road was, figure out which way was north. He could head for Needles—on foot this time. He could do the necessary things—give his warnings, get the research started.

He moved quickly, but with no feeling of triumph this time. He wondered whether Rane and Keira would understand his leaving them. He wondered whether they would forgive him. He knew better than to suppose he would forgive himself.

A jack rabbit leaped into his path, and without thinking, he leaped after it, caught it, snapped its neck. Before he could reflect on what he had done, he heard human footsteps. And before he could take cover in the rocks, someone shot him.

He felt a burning in his left side. Terrified, he dropped the dead rabbit and fled to shelter among the rocks. Moments later, frightened and hurting, he stopped. Someone was following him noisily, perhaps trying to get another clear shot. He concealed himself behind a jagged wedge of rock and waited.

PAST 25

By the time it was certain Jacob Boyd Doyle was not normal, there were two more babies with the same abnormalities.

Jacob never crawled. At six months, he humped along like a big inchworm. Two months later, he began to toddle on all fours, looking disturbingly like a clumsy puppy or kitten. He walked on his hands and feet rather than crawling on hands and knees. With the help of an adult, he could sit up like a dog or cat begging for food. As time passed, he grew strong enough to do this alone. He learned to sit back on his haunches comfortably while using his hands.

He was a beautiful, precocious child, but he was a quadruped. His senses were even keener than those of his parents and his strength would have made him a real problem for parents of only normal strength. And he was a carrier. Eli and Meda did not learn this for certain until later, but they suspected it from the first.

Most important, though, the boy was not human.

Eli could not accept this. Again and again, he tried to teach Jacob to walk upright. A human child walked upright. A boy, a man, walked upright. No son of Eli's would run on all fours like a dog.

Day after day, he kept at Jacob until the little boy sprawled on his stomach and screamed in rebellion.

"Baby, he's too young," Meda said not for the first time. "He doesn't have the balance. His legs aren't strong enough yet."

Chances were, they never would be, and she knew it. She tried to protect the boy from Eli. That shamed and angered Eli so that he could not talk to her about it.

She tried to protect his son from him!

And perhaps Jacob needed her protection. There were times when Eli could not even look at the boy. What in hell was going to happen to a kid who ran around on all fours? A freak who could not hide his strangeness. What kind of life could he have? Even in this isolated section of desert, he might be mistaken for an animal and shot. And what in heaven's name would be done with him if he were captured instead of killed? Would he be sent off to a hospital for "study" or caged and restricted like even the best of the various apes able to communicate through sign language? Or would he simply be stared at, harassed, tormented by normal people? If he spread the disease, it would quickly be traced to him. He would definitely be caged or killed then.

Eli loved the boy desperately, longed to give him the gift of humanity that children everywhere else on earth took for granted. Sometimes Eli sat and watched the boy as he played. At first, Jacob would come over to him and demand attention, even try, Eli believed, to comfort his father or understand his bleakness. Then the boy stopped coming near him. Eli had never turned him away, had even ceased trying to get him to walk upright. In fact, Eli was finally accepting the idea that Jacob would never walk on his hind legs with any more ease or grace than a dog doing tricks. Yet the boy began to avoid him.

Eli was slow in noticing. Not until he called Jacob and saw that the boy cringed away from him did he realize that it had been many days since Jacob had touched him voluntarily.

Many days. How many? Eli thought back.

A week, perhaps. The boy had ceased to come near him or touch him exactly when he began wondering if it were not a cruelty to leave such a hopeless child alive.

PRESENT 26

Rane sat frightened and alone among members of the car family. They had put her on the floor against a wall in what had been the living room of the ranch house. She was still shackled, feeling miserable and tired. Her arms, legs, and back ached with wanting to change position. Once she had inched away from the wall and lain down. The instant she closed her eyes, there was a hand on her left breast and another on her right thigh.

She had sat up quickly and squirmed away from the hands. The car rats had only laughed. They could have raped her. She thought they might eventually. At that moment, they were preoccupied with the ranch women—a mother and her thirteen-year-old daughter. There was also a twelve-year-old son. Rane had heard some of the car rats had raped him, too. She didn't doubt it. They had placed her opposite an open hall door that was directly across from the door of the bedroom-cell of what was left of the ranch family. She could not help seeing occasional car rats going in or out, zipping or unzipping their pants. She could not help hearing moaning, pleading, praying, weeping, screaming whenever the room door was opened. The ranch house was solidly built. Sounds did not carry well unless doors were open. Rane suspected the car rats had put her where she was so that she could see and hear what was in store for her.

They were watching a movie from the ranch family's library —a 1998 classic about the Second Coming of Christ. There had been a whole genre of such films just before the turn of the century. Some were religious, some antireligious, some merely exploitive—Sodom-and-Gomorrah films. Some were cause-oriented—God arrives as a woman or a dolphin or a throwaway kid. And some were science fiction. God arrives from Eighty-two Eridani Seven.

Well, maybe God had arrived a few years late from Proxima Centauri Two. God in the form of a deadly little microbe that for its own procreation made a father try to rape his dying daughter—and made the daughter not mind.

Rane squeezed her eyes shut, willing the tears not to come again, failing. What was worse? Being raped by three or four car rats before she was ransomed or submitting to Eli's people and microbe? Or were the two the same now that the car gang was infected? No, she would probably have been safer back with Stephen Kaneshiro, who could have hurt her but had not, who had tried to share part of himself with her even though she had not understood.

But there was Jacob to think of. All the Jacobs. Stephen Kaneshiro could not give her a human child. It did not matter what the car gang gave her. They would free her as soon as they had the ransom money. Then she could have a doctor take care of the disease and any possible pregnancy. If only the car family did not kill her before the ransom was paid.

Somehow, in spite of the noise from across the hall, in spite of its effect on her, she fell asleep sitting up. If there were more hands, she did not feel them.

When she awoke, she was intensely hungry. The movie was over, and the car rats were shooting and shouting and stinking with sweat so foul she could almost taste it. Her first impulse was to try to drag herself away from them, but her hunger was too intense. Even her head throbbed with it.

She begged the nearest car rat for food, but he shoved her aside with one foot and kept reloading guns as they were passed to him. Most were not passed to him. Their users reloaded them themselves in a couple of seconds. Others were older, slower, more likely to jam. These the reloader handled.

Helplessly, automatically, Rane inched toward the kitchen. She knew where it was. She and Keira had been left in it when they were rescued from their father.

Rane shook her aching head, not wanting to think about that. She did not know where Keira was or what was happening to her. She cared, but she did not want to think about it now. She was not even sure where her father was. She worried about him because he was obviously sick. He might hurt himself and not even know it. The car rats might hurt him because he could not respond to their orders. But as worried as she was about him, she could not keep her mind on him. She was so weak, so sick with hunger, and the kitchen seemed so far away.

She was not sure how far she had gone across the vast room when someone stopped her.

"Where the hell do you think you're going, sis? What's the matter with you?"

"I'm hungry," she gasped.

"Hungry? Shit, you're sick. You're soaking wet."

Rane managed to look up, see that it was a deep-voiced woman who had stopped her, not a man as she had thought. Of course. She smelled like a woman. Rane shook her head, trying to remember whether men and women had always smelled noticeably different. But she could not keep her mind on the question.

"Please," she begged, "just give me some food."

"You're probably not even strong enough to eat."

"Please," Rane wept. She had done more crying in the past few days than she had in the past several years. She could not recall feeling so utterly helpless before. What would happen if the woman prevented her from reaching food? She was already in more pain than she thought could result from hunger.

"You get back to your place and keep from underfoot," the woman said. She was large and blocky. Rane at her best could not have gotten past her. Now, all but helpless, Rane felt herself dragged back to her place at the wall.

"Stay put!" the woman said, then stomped away in her heavy boots. Immediately, Rane began crawling toward the kitchen again. She could not help herself.

She had her hand stepped on once, painfully, and someone shouted at her and cursed her, but no one stopped her again. She reached the kitchen, noticed peripherally that someone had found a gunport there alongside the sink. A bald, shirtless man stood before it, firing mechanically. The man had enough hair on his body to cover several heads.

A gorilla, Rane thought. No more human than the things he was firing at. Jesus, was anyone negotiating with her grandparents or were they all here trying to kill Eli's people? How long had the siege gone on? Two days? Three? More? She could not remember.

She managed to drag herself upright by using the handles of the large refrigerator, then stand while she pulled one of the doors open. There was little food to be found. A few fresh vegetables —tomatoes, a limp carrot, two cucumbers, green onions, green beans.

She ate everything she could find. By the time the shooting let up and the hairy man on the other side of the kitchen had time to pay attention to her, she had opened the other side of the refrigerator and found several steaks probably intended for the night's dinner. The steaks were raw, some of them still icy. There was some cooked meat, too—what was left of a pair of large roasts scraped together onto one platter.

Without thinking, Rane chose the raw meat. Its coldness disturbed her but the fact that it was raw did not even penetrate her consciousness until she had cleaned the bone of the first steak and was beginning the second. Raw smelled better than cooked, that was all.

Finally she began to feel stronger, aware enough for her bloody hands and the bloody meat she held to startle her. She had never liked her meat even medium rare, had always eaten it well-done or, as Keira said, burned. But this meat, except for its coldness, was the best thing she had ever tasted.

Now the car rat saw what she was doing, and, amazed, came to take the second steak from her. She did her best to bite off one of his fingers. If her bound hands and feet had not restricted her movement, she would have succeeded. As it was, her unexpected swiftness and ferocity drove the car rat back.

"Goddamn," he said staring at her as she tore off a piece of steak. "Goddamn, you and your whole family are crazy."

He was an ape. Heavy brow ridges, flattened, broken nose, body hair no one would believe. But now that she had eaten, now that she felt stronger, she realized he smelled interesting.

She finished her steak while he watched, repelled and fascinated. Then she wiped her mouth and smiled. "I won't hurt you," she said, knowing he would laugh.

He laughed humorlessly. "Damn right you won't, sis."

"I was hungry."

"You were crazy—are crazy."

He liked her. She could see it as clearly as though that wary face of his were leering.

"So?" she said, shrugging. "Who the hell isn't crazy these days?" One of her father's patients had said that to her—a young thief with skin as smooth as Keira's except where acid had scarred him. He had been brought to the enclave hospital for special treatment and had laughed at her when she tried to talk him out of leaving the hospital and going back to his gang. He could not get even with the acid thrower, he said, until he was with his own again. This in spite of the fact that his own had run away and left him writhing on the ground.

"You're crazy!" she had screamed at him.

"So who isn't crazy these days?" he had demanded.

"I'm not," she had said. *"And I never will be. Go ahead and flush yourself down the toilet if you want to!"*

Her father had only just begun letting her volunteer at the hospital. The boy's self-destructive stubbornness had upset her, but she had comforted herself with the knowledge that she was stronger than he was. He could have healed completely and gotten work in one of the enclaves. She had told him she would talk her father into helping him. But he had chosen the sewers. She was stronger and smarter.

Or was she merely untested?

She knew the disease organisms were pushing her toward this repulsive man. And she was yielding to them mindlessly. Stephen Kaneshiro had resisted, had not raped her. She could resist, too.

Deliberately, she took another steak. She was not very hungry now, but the meat still smelled good. It was not hard for her to tear into it as messily as possible. She let blood run down her chin and arms, chewed with her mouth open, occasionally smacking her lips. Eventually, she heard the ape make a sound of disgust and stomp away.

The shooting had stopped. Rane was alone in the kitchen— happy to be alone. She thought she might be able to get out the back door if she could get free of her cuffs. She bit pieces of fat from the steak and rubbed them on her wrists. Nothing in the kitchen would be likely to cut the cuffs. Very likely, nothing in the house would cut them. The plastic only looked flimsy. But she thought if she did not fight them, she might be able to slip them. She had seen her father try to do this and fail. But it seemed to her he had not used his muscles effectively, and he had had no fat to help him. She had to try. Anything was better than just sitting and waiting to see what her captors or the disease organism would do to her next.

Several minutes later, as she was freeing one hand through flexibility and control that amazed even her, a young white-haired woman caught her.

If Rane had had time to free her feet, she might have been able to silence the woman before the woman shouted an alarm. As it was, all Rane could do was hop toward her, only to be stopped by the ape who came running to see what was wrong.

The ape grasped her wrists and held them. "Son of a bitch," he said, grinning. "That's the first time I've seen anybody get out of the jail cuffs. Shit, I've tried to get out of a few pair myself. What'd you do, sis?"

He was too close to her. *Too close!* He smelled almost edible. Irresistible. She pressed herself against him.

"Jesus," the white-haired woman said. "What is it with these people?"

"You tell me," the ape said, holding Rane. She rubbed herself against his hairy body, smiling outside and screaming inside. It was as though she were two people. One wanted, needed, was utterly compelled to have this man—perhaps any man. Her hands fumbled with his belt.

Yet some part of her was still *her.* That part screamed, soundlessly weeping, and clawed with imaginary fingers at the ape's ugly, stupid face.

Her true fingers quivered, hesitated for a moment at his belt. Then the organism controlled her completely. Her body moved only under its compulsion and her feelings were abruptly reconciled with her actions. Part of her seemed to die.

"Let her alone," the white-haired woman said. "You can see she's running on empty. Who knows what crazy thing she might do? Besides, we've got to keep her in good shape for the ransom."

And the ape growled, "You worry about yours, Smokey. The buyers for this one will just have to take her back a little used." The ape lifted Rane off her bound feet. "At least this kid is young. What the hell do you want with that sick old man you've got?" He laughed as he carried Rane away into another room.

The new room was not empty. There were people there, writhing together, moaning, making other sounds that Rane paid no attention to. The ape threw her onto an empty bed. There seemed to be several beds in the room. The ape freed her feet, then casually tore her clothing off. Finally, he climbed onto her and hurt her so badly she screamed aloud. But even as she screamed, she knew that what she was doing was *necessary*. She could have hurt him back. He did not realize how vulnerable he was, hunching between her thighs; she could kill him. There was a time, she recalled dimly, when she would have used her advantage. But that time was past. His throat, his eyes, his groin were safe from her. She bore the pain somehow, and when he finished, she lay bleeding, uncaring as he shackled her again. This time he bound her, spread-eagle, to the bed.

Sometime later, there was another man. She did not know him, did not recall having seen him before. He did not hurt her as much. Before he touched her, her body felt almost healed. She did not mind what he did, did not mind the man who came after him. By then, she was aware of her body repairing itself. The organism was taking care of her.

She lost track of time, of the men. Once when she began to feel hungry, she asked the man who was with her for food. He laughed at her, but later he brought her food—raw meat and raw vegetables. He unshackled her and watched in amazement and disgust as she ate. Several people had come to watch. They smelled unwashed and wary, but since they did not bother her, she ignored them.

When someone tried to shackle her again, she resisted. There was, it seemed to her now, too much danger in being tied to a bed—or tied at all. She was stronger now, more aware of what was going on around her.

In one corner, a young boy, naked, covered with blood, lay like discarded trash. He did not move. He had clearly been tortured, mutilated. His hands were still shackled. She was certain he was dead, had probably bled to death. His ears and his penis had been cut off.

The woman on the bed near her had been crying hoarsely. Now, filthy, bound spread-eagle across a small bed, she was unconscious. Rane could see and hear her breathing shallowly.

A young girl, tied across another bed, lay watching what

happened to Rane. The girl's wrists and ankles were bleeding in spite of the relative gentleness of the security cuffs. Her body was bruised and bloody and there was something wrong about her eyes.

Abruptly, the girl gave a long, shrill scream. No one was touching her or paying any attention to her, but she continued to scream until one of the men went over and slapped her. Then she was abruptly, completely silent.

"I don't want to be tied," Rane said gravely to the man who was struggling to hold her arms. She realized that she was having no trouble avoiding the cuffs. The man seemed weaker than the others who had handled her—though he did not look weaker. Perhaps she was stronger.

Other people laughed when she spoke, but the man trying to tie her did not. "Help me," he said. "She's as strong as a goddamn truck! She's playing with me!"

She was not playing. Abruptly, as a second man seized her, she thrust both away and got up. She was still naked, as dirty and bloody as the young girl. But she was beginning to understand that she was stronger. Perhaps she was not as strong as she would be. She thought not. But she was stronger than anyone would expect her to be—strong enough to escape. Even getting away naked would be better than staying here, having her organisms keep her alive while the car rats thought up new things to do to her.

A black woman with red hair leveled one of the newer automatic rifles at her as she fought off a second attacker. When she saw the gun, she thought she was dead. But at that moment, she heard shouts through the open door.

"Hey, Badger," someone yelled, "the old man is gone. He kicked out his window!"

"Huh!" the red-haired woman said. "Nobody could kick out one of these windows alone. He'd have to kick out half the wall. Somebody must have helped him!" And as an afterthought, "Where's Smoke?"

Her father was gone.

He had escaped! He had used his new strength and gotten away! And what about Keira? Perhaps she had gotten away, too. People tended not to pay much attention to her because she looked too frail to try anything. But maybe . . .

Rane lunged at the redhead. The woman's attention had been drawn away from Rane. Now, she seemed to react in slow motion as Rane moved.

Rane seized the gun, swatted the woman on the side of her head with the stock, then swung the gun around on the other car rats. Two-hundred-round magazine, fully loaded, set on automatic. A couple of seconds passed, then someone laughed. Maybe a naked girl holding a rifle looked funny. Let them laugh.

Someone made a grab for the barrel. That was a degree of stupidity Rane had not expected. She fired, managed to shoot only the man whose hand had brought the gun to bear on his own belly. She resisted the urge to spray the whole group.

The wounded man screamed, doubled over, fell to the floor. Rane stepped back from him quickly, looking to see whether anyone else was feeling suicidal. As it happened, no one else was armed. People did not come to this room with their guns.

Nobody moved.

"Get your clothes off," Rane told one of the smaller women.

The woman understood. She stripped quickly, threw her clothing to Rane, glanced sideways at the rat bleeding and groaning on the floor. The red-haired woman had knelt beside him, trying to stop the bleeding with direct pressure.

"Get the hell out of here," Rane said. "All of you, out!"

They spilled through the doorway ahead of her and she followed close behind, hoping her speed would give her an edge over their numbers and organization. She barely paused to snatch up the discarded clothing. She could dress when she was safe, when she had joined her father and they were on their way to Needles again.

She darted out the door, across the hall, across the large living room. She could see reaction around her, but it was so slow, she knew how fast she must be moving.

But there was noise outside. Motors, vehicles approaching,

people shouting. This was what she had distracted attention from. New car people arriving. New car rats on the outside where she had to go. They were already shooting, fighting with Eli's people. More crossfire for her to be caught in.

She put her back against the wall near the front door and aimed her gun at one of the car rats.

"Open this door," she said.

"I can't," he lied. "It needs a special key." It could not have been more obvious to her that he was lying if he had worn a sign.

She fired a short burst, and he fell. Now the screaming inside her returned. She was shooting people, killing people. She was going to be a doctor someday. Doctors did not kill people; they helped people heal. Her father had carried a gun for years and never shot anyone. He had escaped without shooting anyone.

But she could not.

The instant she showed indecision, weakness, mercy, these people would cut her to pieces. In this room several were as formidably armed as she was. All she had going for her was terrifying speed and perhaps their belief that they would soon be rid of her one way or another without anyone playing hero. Nothing she had ever heard about rat packs gave any indication they were heroic. At best, they mistook ruthlessness for heroism.

"Open the door," she said to a second man.

He stumbled quickly to obey.

"You!" she chose a third. "Help him!"

"He doesn't need any hel— No!"

She had come within a hair of shooting him. He scurried to the first man, then stood by while the first opened the door.

Of course, the instant the door moved, Eli's people opened fire at it. Someone—one of the new group of car rats, perhaps—managed to run onto the porch, but did not quite make it to the door.

Rane heard all this as she ran from the room. She had never intended to step into the battle at the front of the house. She would never have headed for the front if she had known what was going on there. Once there, however, she had to create a diversion so that she could get to the back door.

Someone shot at her as she ran, but she was too quick. In the kitchen, she stopped, turned, fired a short burst at the door she had just run through. That should stop any pursuit. She hesitated, saw a flash of color at the door, sprayed the doorway again. Then she went to the back door. If it required a key, she might be trapped. That depended on how thoroughly bulletproof the house was.

Her hand flew over the various locks that did not require keys. She had to shoot the last one off, though at least it came off. As she fired, however, someone else fired at her, hit her in the lower back.

She fell to her knees, tried to swing around, but was shot again. This time, the impact of the bullet spun her around. She held on to her rifle somehow and managed to spray the other side of the room. She heard screaming, knew she had hit something.

She released the trigger only when, briefly, through a haze, she thought she saw her sister staring at her over a counter, through a doorway. Then, because she was propped up against the door, unable to move her legs—unable even to feel her legs, she sprayed the last of her bullets into the car rats as they showed themselves. She had the satisfaction of seeing the ape fall before someone shot her again.

The disease organism was merciless. It kept her alive even when she knew she must be almost cut in half. It kept her conscious and aware of everything up through the moment someone stood over her, shouting, then seized her by the hair and held her head up as he began to saw slowly at her throat with something dull.

PAST 27

The women had become frightened of Eli—frightened for their children. Gwyn's daughter by Eli was beginning to toddle around on all fours and Lorene's daughter by Zeriam clearly had the same physical abnormalities. She would be another quadruped, another precocious, strong, beautiful, little nonhuman. Eli could see that. He watched the children in grim silence.

The women sat Eli down and talked to him. Gwyn spoke for them all for a change while Meda sat withdrawn and silent.

"We don't like being afraid of you," Gwyn said, leaning forward against the dining table around which they had gathered. "We need you." She glanced sideways at Meda. "And we love you. But we're afraid."

"Afraid of what?" he demanded harshly. He did not care what the women had to say. His own misery over the children consumed him.

"You know of what," Gwyn said. "Even the kids know. They don't understand, but they're scared to death of you."

He stared at her in bitter anger. She had brought the others together against him. They had never united against him before. He was father or foster father to all three kids—all three hopelessly nonhuman kids. No one had the right to tell him how he should feel about them.

"Eli, you love them," Meda whispered finally. "You love them all. You'd have to go against your deepest feelings to hurt them."

"We won't let you hurt them," Lorene said.

"We can't change them," Gwyn said. "And no matter how you feel . . . if you try to hurt them, we'll kill you."

Eli stared at her, amazed. She was the gentlest of the three women, the one most likely to need reassurance and want protection.

"*We will kill you,*" she repeated very softly. She did not flinch from his gaze. He looked at Meda and Lorene and saw Gwyn's feelings mirrored in their faces.

He reached across the table, took Gwyn's hands. "I can't help what I feel," he said. "I know it hurts you. It hurts *me*. But—"

"It scares us!"

"I know." He paused. "What in this world is going to happen to kids with human minds and four legs? Think about it!"

"Who says they have human minds?" Meda asked.

Eli glared at her.

"They're obviously bright," she said, "but their minds may be as different as their bodies. We can teach them, but we can't know ahead of time what they'll become."

"No," he said. "We can't. But we know the world they'll have to spend their lives in. And I know what their lives will be like if they can't fit in—and, of course, there's no way they can fit in. You think sewers and cesspools are bad? Try a cage. Bars, you know. Locks."

"Nobody would—"

"Shit! They're not going to be cute little kids forever. To other people, they wouldn't look like cute little kids now. And we're not going to live forever to protect them."

The women stared at him bleakly.

"I'll tell you something else," he said. "These kids are only the first. You *know* there'll be more. If anything happened to me, you'd go out and find yourselves another man or two. Hell, you'll do that even if nothing happens to me. We'll probably bring in more women, too. Our organism won't let us ignore all those uninfected people out there completely."

No one contradicted him. The women could feel the truth of what he was saying as intensely as he could.

"What are we doing?" Lorene whispered. "What are we creating?"

Eli leaned back, eyes closed. "That's what I've been asking myself," he said. "I've got an answer now."

They all faced him, waiting. He realized then that he loved them. He wondered when he had begun to love them—three plain women with calluses on their hands. Answering them would not be an act of love, but it was necessary. If anyone deserved to know what he thought, they did. "We're the future," he said simply. "We're the sporangia of the dominant life form of Proxi Two—the receptacles that produce the spores of that life form. If we survive, *if our children survive*, it will be because we fulfill our purpose—because we spread the organism."

"Spread the disease?" Lorene asked

"Yes."

"Deliberately? I mean . . . to everybody? After you said—"

"I didn't say we should spread it deliberately. I didn't say we *should* spread it at all. I said we won't survive, and the kids won't survive, if we don't. But I'll tell you, I don't think they or we are in any real danger. Once we knew what to look for on Proxi Two, we found the organism in almost every animal species alive there. Some were immune—herbivores tended to be immune—and though I can't prove it, I suspect a lot of species had been driven into extinction."

"Some would be here," Lorene said. "Dogs."

Eli nodded. "Dogs, yes, maybe coyotes, wolves, any canine. I wouldn't give much for the chances of cats either, and some snakes—maybe all snakes, rats, most rodents. Heaven knows what else."

"What about the people?" Lorene whispered. "They'll die, too. Four out of seven died here. Five, if you count Gwyn's baby.

Ten out of fourteen in your crew died. And what about Andy? How many more Andy Zeriams, Eli?" She had begun to cry. "How goddamn many?"

He got up and went to her. She pushed him away angrily at first, but then reached out and pulled him to her.

"What about the people?" she repeated against him.

After a moment, he put her aside and sat down next to Meda.

"What do you want to do?" Meda asked.

He shook his head. "Nothing. Just go on as we have."

"But—"

"What else? You're right about the kids. They are what they are. I'm right too. They can't make it in the world as it is. But I'm not going to make a move to spread the disease beyond the ranch, here. Not even for them. We'll have to bring people here now and then, but that's all."

"You're talking about leaving everything to chance," Meda said.

"No," he told her, "not quite. I'm talking about stifling chance, doing every damn thing I can to keep the disease right here. Everything. And I'll need all three of you with me."

"But the kids," Meda said.

"Yeah." He sighed. "I couldn't hurt them. Even without the three of you ganging up on me, I couldn't have. But . . . in this one way, I can't help them, either. Can you?" He looked from one of them to the other. No one answered. "What happens happens," Eli continued. "I won't make it happen. Dead people, dead animals, no more cities because we'd go crazy in cities. No more of a lot of things I probably haven't even thought of." He stared at the table for several seconds.

"It will happen, though," he said. "Sooner or later, somehow, it will happen. And ultimately, I'll be responsible."

PRESENT 28

Keira had just eaten a large meal—overcooked, overseasoned, but filling. She was feeling well until the white-haired girl came to take her to her father. She was feeling *well!* She could not remember how long it had been since she had last felt truly well.

The car family had locked her in a walk-in hall closet. She had been in pain and Badger had demanded to know why. When she told him she had leukemia, he had shrugged.

"So?" he had said. "There's a cure for that—some kind of medicine that makes the bad cells turn back to normal."

"I've had that," she told him. "It didn't work."

"What do you mean, it didn't work? It works. It worked on my mother. She had the same shit you do."

"It didn't work on me."

So he had locked her in the closet. Some of his people, ignorant and fearful, could not quite believe her illness was not contagious. Badger locked her away from them for her own safety. She had seen for herself how eager they were to get her out of their sight. She wondered what they would do if they knew what she and her family had really given them—what they were really doomed to. They would begin to find out soon enough. That was what Eli was waiting for. That was why he was keeping them boxed in. He did not have to do anything more than that to win. She had heard him talking about explosives, but then the car family had begun showing a noisy movie and the faint voices from outside were drowned.

Yet there were explosives. Eli would do anything necessary to stop the car people if they threatened to break free before they were ready to join him. He certainly would not let the friends they had called reach them. Keira did not know what would happen to her, but somehow she was not afraid. She sat on the closet floor with bound hands and feet, reading from cardboard boxes of old magazines. The lavish use of paper fascinated her. A one-hundred-dred-and-twenty page magazine for only five or six dollars. A collector's item. Computer libraries like her father's made more sense, occupied less space, could be more easily updated, but somehow, weren't as much fun to look at.

The light in the closet was dim, but Keira preferred it dim. She thought she might not be able to tolerate it if it were normally bright. She was looking through an old *National Geographic* when the white-haired girl opened the door.

"Your father wants to see you," the girl said in her low, throaty voice.

Keira looked up from her magazine, stared at the girl, wondered what it might be like to be her—dirty, knowing, tough, headed nowhere, but still young and not bad-looking. The girl's dark-tanned skin contrasted oddly with her white hair.

"He might want to see my sister," Keira said, "but I don't think he wants to see me."

"You the one he had the fight with?" the girl asked.

Keira did not hesitate. "Yes."

"Doesn't matter. He just wants to see one of you to make sure we haven't shot you. Come on." She unfastened Keira's hand and leg restraints.

Keira started to refuse. She did not think the girl would force her. Then she realized that in spite of what had happened between them, she wanted to see her father—probably for the same reason he wanted to see her. Just to be sure he was all right. He had seemed so weak and sick when she saw him last. The organism seemed to be making her strong and him weak. That was all that had permitted her to get away from him when Rane made her realize what was happening.

It occurred to her that as things stood now, each time she saw him might be the last. The thought frightened her and she tried to reject it, but it had taken hold.

"All right," she said, standing up.

The girl watched her intently. "Is he really your father?"

"Yes."

"Is he part black, then, or is it just your mother?"

"My mother was black. He's white."

The girl nodded. "My mother was from Sweden. God knows why she came here. Got raped her first week here. That's where I came from."

Shocked, Kiera spoke the first words that occurred to her. "But why didn't she have an—" Keira stopped, glanced downward. There was something wrong with asking someone why she had not been aborted. She wondered why the girl would tell her such a secret, shameful thing.

"She couldn't make up her mind," the girl said unperturbed. "She wanted to get rid of me, then she didn't, then she wasn't sure, then I was born and it was too late. She kept me 'til I was fourteen, though. Then she went nuts and when they took her away to cure her, I left." The girl sighed. "After that, life was shit until I got adopted into the family. How old are you?"

"Sixteen," Keira told her.

"Really? How old is he?"

Keira looked at her sharply. The girl looked away. For a moment, Keira hated her, wanted to get away from her. Her rage surprised her, then shamed her because she could not help understanding its cause: jealousy. The girl had slept with Blake—as Keira herself almost had. His scent was on her like a signature. For a moment Keira wondered how she could distinguish such a thing. His scent . . . Yet there was no doubt in her mind, and she was almost stiff with jealous rage.

Then came the shame.

"Forty-four," she said softly. "He's forty-four." Neither she nor the girl said anything more. The girl let Keira in to see her father, then minutes later, let her out again. Only then could she look at the girl and realize her father needed an ally among the car people. The girl liked him and she could be useful to him in ways Keira certainly could not.

"Forty-four isn't old," Keira said as the girl took her back to the closet.

The girl glanced at her. "What'd you do? Decide it was okay for me to fuck him?"

Keira jumped. Not for the first time, she was grateful she was not as light-skinned as Rane. Nothing made Rane blush. Everything would have made Keira blush.

"I just thought you liked him," Keira muttered.

"What if I do? He's your father, not the other way around."

Keira tried once more. "Did you bring him the blanket?" she asked. "And food?" She had seen an empty plate on the floor near him.

"Yeah, so what?"

"Thank you," Keira said sincerely. She went back into the closet, waited to see whether the girl would put the cuffs back on her. But the girl only looked at her, then closed the door. Keira waited for the soft click of the lock, but did not hear it. Moments later, she heard the girl's footsteps going away.

Keira was almost free. With her enhanced senses, she might be able to slip out of the house, escape.

Alone.

But the white-haired girl had given her a choice she did not want—to challenge the car family by attempting to escape, to desert her own family, or to remain in dangerous captivity. Here, she certainly could not help her family. At any time, Badger might decide to kill his captives, rape them, use them as shields, anything. He had kicked her father almost into unconsciousness for no reason at all. He and his people were unpredictable, ruthless, and, worst of all, cornered. What would happen when they began to realize they were sick as well?

And whatever they decided to do, how would her staying affect them? Would it stop them from doing harm? Of course not.

But if she escaped, the gang might take their anger and frustration out on her father and Rane. She hooked her arms around her knees, pulled her knees up close to her chest. There she sat miserably as though she were still bound, still locked in.

Each time she thought of her father, her mind flinched away, then fastened onto him again, forcing her into memories of the thing that had almost happened—into confusion, fear, shame, loss, desire. . . .

Then she would remember the way Eli had looked at her, the feel of his body along the length of her own and inside her, hurtful, but good somehow. That would not happen again. Meda would be there and Keira's father would not. Eli would steer her toward someone else; he had warned her. That hurt, but it could not matter.

She listened intently for several seconds, heard the movie end, heard the shooting flare up and die down. Down the hall, people were making love—or the ranch women were being raped. She had heard a little of that before and did not want to hear more. There were people wandering around, talking, firing occasionally at targets they probably could not see. Someone was talking about eating raw meat.

The words made her mouth water. Her hunger was not painful yet, but it would be soon. Nothing else was hurting her body now, but hunger could change that quickly. If she waited much longer, let herself be locked in again, she could starve. The car gang would not understand. It might ignore her. This closet could become her tomb.

She grasped the knob, turned it slowly, noiselessly. She heard nothing nearby—not even breathing.

Yet the instant she opened the door, something small, silent, and incredibly quick leaped into the closet with her. Only her speeded-up reaction time saved her. Her moment of confusion and terror passed so quickly, she was able to keep herself from screaming. Instead, she shut the closet door quickly, quietly, and turned to face Jacob.

He was naked and trembling. Before she realized what he meant to do, he leaped again, this time at her.

To her amazement, she caught him. He was heavy, but she had no trouble holding him. A few days before, she did not think she could have lifted him from the ground, let alone caught him in midair. He clung to her, utterly silent, but clearly terrified.

"What are you *doing* here?" she whispered, hugging him and rubbing his trembling shoulders. She was surprised to realize how glad she was to see him—and how frightened she was for him in this deadly place. "Jacob, you could get hurt! You could get—" She stopped. "You have to get away!"

"You do, too," he said. "Nobody knew where you were in the house so I came to find you. Everybody from home is outside."

"Do your parents know you're inside?"

"No!" He drew back from her a little, his trembling quieted. "Don't tell them. Okay?"

"I won't tell them a thing. Just let's get out of here. How did you get in?"

"There's a room with a hole instead of window glass. You were in there before. It smells like you—and like other people."

"A room with a hole?"

Distantly, Keira heard shooting and running feet. It sounded like fighting within the house. Car people fighting among themselves.

Jacob glanced toward the door. "They were hurting her," he said. "She's got a gun and shot one of them. Now she's shooting more."

"Who?"

"Your sister. She's getting away."

"Is she? My God, let's go!"

"Your father's gone, too, I think. I smelled the room where he was back at home. His same smell was in the room with the hole."

God, while she had sat worrying about leaving them, they were leaving her. She opened the door, crept out of the closet, still holding the boy.

"I'll show you where the hole is," he said. He squirmed against her, leaped soundlessly to the floor, sped down the hall toward her father's room. Of course the hole would be there. But how had her father broken out the glass?

And Rane. Was she all right? Could she make it alone? Keira turned, crept back up the hall to the family room. This room adjoined the kitchen and the dining room. From the hall door of the family room, Keira could see car people crouched behind the counter, occasionally looking around or over it into the kitchen. Keira could see over the counter and into the kitchen, could see Rane sitting at the back door, cradling an automatic rifle. For an instant, Rane's eyes met Keira's. Then Jacob was tugging at Keira's dress.

"Go!" Keira whispered. "Get out!"

"You come too," the boy pleaded. "The whole house smells like blood. People are dying."

Rane began firing again, and people did die. Keira saw one of them raise his head at the wrong time and get the top of it blown off.

Terrified and repelled, Keira snatched up Jacob and fled. Doctor's daughter that she was, sick as she had been, she had never seen anyone die before. She ran almost in panic, reached her father's bare room and looked around wildly.

"There!" The boy pointed to another door. The bathroom —no bigger than the closet she had been shut in, but it had a window.

She ran into the bathroom, shut the door and locked it, then lifted the boy to the windowsill. He was over it and down in an instant. She pulled herself up after him, no longer marveling at the return of her strength, no longer marveling at anything. She had to get out of the house, get back to Eli and safety. Her father was probably already safe, and Rane soon would be.

She dropped to the ground and ran.

Keira ran through the rocks, hoping they would conceal and protect her as she circled around the house. She was halfway around and already aware of the distinctive scent of Eli's people when she recognized another familiar scent. The new scent confused her for a moment because of its clarity. She was so utterly certain it was her father's that for a moment she thought she had actually seen him.

The wind favored her. It blew toward her from Eli's people and across the path of her father. She looked down the slope through the rocks. Her nose told her this was the way her father had gone—away from the house and Eli's people, toward the highway.

Of course.

Her enhanced sense of smell led her to spots of his blood, some of them still wet on the rocks. In one place near a brown wedge of rock, blood had actually pooled—an alarming amount of blood. Before finding this, she had thought she would go on to Eli and say nothing about her father. Jacob, running ahead and back to her like an eager puppy, might notice the scent and he might not. If he spoke of it, she would have to admit what she knew, but perhaps by then her father would have made good his escape. She would have let him escape, even knowing what that would mean to Eli and his people. This was all she could do for her father. And in his way, he was not wrong. He was taking the long view, trying to prevent a future epidemic. Eli and his people were trying to live from one day to the next, trying to raise their strange children in peace, trying to control their deadly compulsion. Eventually, inevitably, they would fail. They must have known it. If not for the blood, Keira would have deliberately permitted that failure to happen now.

But the blood was there, slowly drying in a natural depression in the rock. Her father had been hurt, needed help. Eli had the medical bag, maybe even had it with him here to treat his own people. He should not be able to use it, but Keira suspected he could—and her father might die before he could reach other help.

She turned aside to follow the blood trail. The next time Jacob raced back to her, approaching in utter silence, and concealed except for his scent until the last instant, she stopped him.

"Come on," he said. "I'll take you to where Daddy is."

"You go," she said. "Tell him my father's hurt and I have to find him. Tell him to send someone after me with my father's bag. Okay?"

"Yes."

"Good. Now go. And be careful."

The boy bounded away, leaping among the rocks as though they presented no obstacle at all. Her children would do that someday. They would have four legs and be able to bound like cats, and they would be beautiful. Perhaps she was already pregnant.

Somehow, when she found her father, when Eli helped him, he had to be convinced to stay and be quiet. *He had to be!* Living day to day, free on the desert was better than being a quarantined guinea pig in some hospital or lab, better than watching Jacob and Zera treated like little animals, better than perhaps being sterilized so that no more children like them could be born. Better than vanishing.

She ran down the rocky slope with new speed and agility she hardly noticed. It seemed she could always see a place for her feet, always find a handhold when one was necessary. She felt as secure as a mountain goat. Once she stopped to examine the body of a red-bearded, balding man. He was not one of Eli's people, not one of Badger's. Most likely, he was one of the new group Badger had called. He was newly dead of a broken neck. Her father's scent was especially strong near him, and she realized her father had probably killed this man. It was even possible that this was the man who had wounded her father—though she saw no gun. Perhaps her father had taken it. That would mean she had to be careful. If he were wounded and armed, he might be panicky enough to shoot without waiting to see who he was shooting at.

She continued down the slope with greater care. She did not have Eli's or Jacob's ability to move in complete silence, but she moved as quietly as she could, missing the rock and sand she could have knocked loose, avoiding the dry plants that would crackle underfoot, quieting her own panting.

She paused briefly to listen. The wind, now blowing toward her from her father, brought her the sound of his uneven footsteps. He was limping slightly. His breathing, though, was even, not labored. She marveled for a moment that she could actually hear his breathing over such a distance. The organism had given her a great deal. It must have given him something too. How else could he survive being shot and losing so much blood? How else could he keep going? If only something could be done to stop it from killing so many people while it helped others.

She became aware of a low rumble behind her. Looking back, she saw a truck—a big private hauler—probably carrying something illegal if it were daring to use a map-identified sewer. She dove for cover as the truck came over a rise. Perhaps the driver was in his living quarters and would not see her or her father. Perhaps. But what driver would leave his rig on automatic in a sewer? He would be at the wheel. And his truck would be armed and armored to fight off gangs and the police.

The truck rumbled past her, not even slowing in spite of the fact that the rock she had crouched behind was not large enough to conceal her completely. Unmoving as she was, perhaps the driver had seen her as just another lump of rock.

But up ahead, beyond the hill that now concealed her father, the truck slowed and stopped. Frightened, she walked toward the truck, then ran toward it. People traveling legitimately did not stop to pick up strays, did not dare. Her father had told her of a time when a person could stand with his thumb held in a certain position, and cars and trucks would stop and offer rides. But Keira could not remember such a time. All her life, she had heard stories of strays being decoys for car families and bike gangs. Real strays were people with car trouble and without working phones or people thrown out of cars by friends who suddenly became less friendly. People who picked them up might be only dangerously naïve or they might be thieves, murderers, traffickers in prostitutes, or, most frighteningly, body-parts dealers—though according to her father, involuntary transplant donors were more likely to come from certain of the privately run, cesspool hospitals. But for a freelancer, strays were fair game.

Keira ran, not knowing what she would do when she reached her father and the hauler, not thinking about it. All she could think was that her father might be shot with a tranquilizer gun and loaded onto a meat truck.

Suddenly, as she ran, there was an explosion, then several

explosions. For a moment, she stopped, confused, and the ground shook under her feet.

The ranch house. Eli had done what she had feared he would do: triggered his explosives, blown up the car people—even the white-haired one who had been kind.

And Rane? Had she gotten out? Was that why Eli had decided to settle things? Or was it because Keira and her father had escaped so easily? Eli almost certainly did not have enough people to surround the house *and* fight the new gang. Were two escapees all he was willing to risk?

Black smoke and dust boiled up over the hills. Keira stared at it, frightened, wondering. Then she heard the hauler start and saw it begin to pull away.

Again, she ran toward her father, pushing herself, fearing to find nothing where he had been. Instead, she found her father half-crushed by the wheels of the truck. His legs, the whole lower half of him looked stuck to the broken pavement with blood and ruined flesh. He could not possibly be alive with such massive injuries.

Her father groaned. Keira dropped down beside him, sickened, revolted. She could barely look at him, yet he was alive.

"God," he whispered. "My God!"

Weeping, Keira took his hand. It was wet with blood and she touched it carefully, but it was uninjured. Clutched in it was a piece of blue cloth—a bloody sleeve, not his own.

"I did it," he moaned. "Oh Jesus, I did it."

"Daddy?" She wanted to put his head on her lap, but she was afraid she would hurt him more.

"Kerry, is that you?" He seemed to be looking right at her.

"It's me."

"I did it. Jesus!"

"Did what?" She could not think. She could hardly talk through her tears.

"He was looking for my wallet . . . or something to steal. He hit me deliberately . . . had to swerve to hit me. Just wanted to steal."

She shook her head in disbelief. She had never heard of

haulers running people down to rob them. Car families were more likely to do that. But in a sewer, anything could happen.

"I grabbed him," her father said. "I couldn't help it, couldn't control it. He smelled so . . . I couldn't help it. God, I tore at him like an animal."

So like the blue sleeve, the blood on his hand was not his. He had spread the disease.

"Please," he pleaded. "Go after him. Stop him."

"Stop who?" Eli asked.

She had not heard him coming. Enhanced senses or not, she stood up, startled. Then she saw her father's bag in his hand. She knew how utterly useless it would be and she broke down.

Crying, she permitted Eli to take her by the shoulders and move her aside. He knelt where she had been. When she was able to see clearly again, she saw that he was holding her father's bloody hand. She felt that something happened between them, a moment of nonverbal communication.

Then, with a long, slow sigh, her father closed his eyes. Eventually he opened them again widely. His chest ceased to move with his breathing. His body was still. Eli reached up and closed the eyes a final time.

Keira knelt beside her father, beside Eli. She looked at Eli, not able to speak to him, not wanting to hear him speak, though she knew he would.

"He's dead," Eli said. "I'm sorry."

She knew. She had seen. She bent forward, crying, all but screaming in anguished protest. With her eyes closed, she could not imagine her father dead. She did not know how to deal with such an unimaginable thing.

Eli took off his shirt and covered the most damaged parts of her father's body. Blood soaked through at once, but at least the horrible injuries were hidden.

Eli stood up, took her hands, and drew her to her feet. Her hands tingled, almost burned where he touched her. Confused, she tried to pull away, but somehow her desire to pull away did not reach her hands. They did not move.

"Be still," he said. "I just went through this with your father.

His organisms 'knew' something mine want to know. So do yours."

That made no sense to her, but she did not care. She was not being hurt. She did not think she would have noticed if he had hurt her. She was still trying to understand that her father was dead. Eli kept talking. Eventually, she found herself listening to him.

"When we've changed," he said, "when the organism 'decides' whether or not we're going to live, it shares the differences it's found in us with others who have changed. At least that's what we've decided it's doing. We had a woman who had had herself sterilized before we got her—had her tubes cauterized. Her organisms communicated with Meda's and her tubes opened up. She's pregnant now. We had a guy regrow three fingers he'd lost years ago. You . . . There's no precedent for it, but I think you may be getting rid of your leukemia. Or maybe the organism's even found a way to use leukemia to its advantage—and yours. You're going to live."

"I should die," she whispered. "Dad was strong and he died."

"You're not going to die. You look healthier than you did when I met you."

"I *should* die!"

"Jesus, I'm glad you're not going to. That makes up for a lot."

She said nothing.

"Kerry?"

"Don't call me that!" she screamed.

"I'm sorry." He put his arm around her as soon as he could free his hands from hers—as soon as the organisms had finished their communication. How the hell could microorganisms communicate anyway, she wondered obscurely.

Eli answered as though she had asked the question aloud. Perhaps she had. "We exchanged something," he said. "Maybe chemical signals of some kind. That's the only answer I can come up with. We've talked about it at home and nobody has any other ideas."

She did not understand why he was talking on and on about the organism. Did he think she cared? Out of the corner of her eye, she saw the column of smoke from the ranch house and she thought of something she did care about.

"Eli?"

"Yeah?"

"What about Rane?"

Silence.

"Eli? Did she get out?"

More silence.

"You blew up the house with her inside!"

"No."

"You did! You killed my sister!"

"Keira!" He turned her, made her face him. "I didn't. We didn't."

She believed him. She did not understand why she believed so quickly, why watching him speak the words made her know he was telling the truth. She resented believing him.

"What happened to her?" she demanded. "Where is she?"

Eli hesitated. "She's dead."

Another one. Another death. Everyone was dead. She was alone.

"The car people killed her," Eli said.

"How could you know that?"

"Keira, I know. And you know I'm not lying to you."

"How could you know she was dead?"

He sighed. "Baby . . ." He drew another breath. "They cut her head off, and they threw it out the front door."

She broke away from him, stumbled a few steps down the road.

"I'm sorry," he said for the third time. "We tried to save all of you. We . . . we work hard not to lose people in the middle of their conversions."

"You're like our children at that stage," another voice said.

She looked up, saw that a young oriental man had come over the hill behind her.

The man spoke to Eli. "I came to see if you needed help. I guess not."

Eli shrugged. "Take her back to the camp. I'll bring her father."

The man took Keira's arm. "I knew your sister," he said softly. "She was a strong girl."

Not strong enough, Keira thought. Not against the car family. Not against the disease. Not strong at all.

She started to follow the new man back to the ranch house, then stopped. She had forgotten something—something important. It must have been important if it could bother her now. Then she remembered.

"Eli?" she said.

He was bending over her father. He straightened when she spoke.

"Eli, someone got away. The hauler who hit my father. He was headed north."

"It was a private hauler?"

"Yes. He got out and tried to rob my father. My father scratched him."

"Oh, Jesus," Eli whispered. He sounded almost the way her father had at the end. Then he turned and spoke to the other man. "Steve, tell Ingraham. He's our best driver. Give him some grenades. Tell him no holds barred."

The man called Steve went leaping up the slope as agilely as Jacob could have.

"Jesus," Eli repeated. Somehow, he managed to lift her father and carry him back as though he were merely wounded, not half-crushed. He had fashioned a kind of sack of his shirt. Keira walked beside him, hardly noticing when a car sped by down on the highway.

Up the hill, Steve—Stephen Kaneshiro, he told her—joined her again. He brought her food and she ate ravenously, guiltily. Apparently nothing would disturb her appetite.

Stephen kept her away from the ruin of the house. He stayed with her, silent but somehow comforting. He found an empty car and sat with her in it. Eli's people had apparently driven away or killed all of the second, uncontaminated group of car people. Now they were cleaning up. Some were digging a mass grave. Others were loading their newly appropriated cars and trucks with whatever they thought their enclave could use.

"Take a couple of radios," Stephen told a woman who passed near them. "I think for a change we'll be needing them."

The woman nodded and went away.

Jacob found Stephen and Keira sitting together in the car. Without a word, he climbed into Keira's lap and fell asleep. She stroked his hair, accepting his presence and his youth and thinking nothing. It was possible to endure if she thought nothing at all.

Sometime later, Ingraham returned. He had driven all the way to the edge of Needles, but found no private hauler. Everyone had gathered near him to hear about his chase. When they had heard, they all looked at Eli.

Eli closed his eyes, rubbed a hand over his face. "All right." He spoke so softly, Keira would not have heard him without her newly enhanced hearing. "All right, we knew it would happen sooner or later."

"But a private hauler," Stephen said. "They go all over the country, all over the continent. And they deal with people who go all over the world."

Eli nodded bleakly. He looked years older and agonizingly weary.

"What are we going to do?" Ingraham asked.

Meda answered him. "What do you think we're going to do? We're going home!"

Eli put his arm around her. "That's right," he said. "In a few months we'll be one of the few sane enclaves left in the country —maybe in the world. He shook his head. "Use your imagination. Think of what it will be like in the cities and towns." He paused, reached down and picked up Zera, who had sat at his feet and was leaning sideways against his right leg. "Remember the kids," he said softly. "They'll need us more than ever now. Whatever you do, remember the kids."

EPILOGUE

Stephen Kaneshiro waited until he began to hear radio reports of the new illness. Then he put on his gloves and drove with Ingraham into Barstow. From there, by phone, he tried to locate his wife and son. He had been with Keira until then, had seemed content with her, but he felt he had a duty to bring his wife and son to relative safety, though they must have given him up for dead long ago.

Eli warned him that no one knew what effect the disease might have on a young child. Stephen understood, but he wanted to give his family what he felt might be their only chance.

He could not. It took him two days of anonymous, sound-only phoning to discover that his wife had gone back to her parents and recently had returned with them to Japan.

He came back to the mountaintop ranch and Keira. Her hair was growing in thick and dark. She was pregnant—perhaps by Stephen, perhaps from her one night with Eli. Stephen did not seem to care which any more than she did.

"Will you stay with me?" she asked him. He was a good man. He had helped her through the terrible time after the deaths of her father and sister. He did not excite her as Eli had. She had not known how much she cared for him, how much she needed him until he went away. When he came back, all she could think was: *No wife! Thank God!* Then she was ashamed. Sometime later she asked the question.

"Will you stay with me?"

They sat in their room next to the nursery. Their room in Meda's house. He sat on the bed and she on the desk chair where she could not touch him. She could not bear to touch him until she knew he did not plan to leave her.

"We'll have to cut ourselves off even more than we have so far," he said. "I brought new weapons, ammunition, and foods we can't raise. I think we're going to have to be self-sufficient for a while. Maybe a long while. You and I couldn't even have a house. Not enough wood."

"It doesn't matter," she said.

"San Francisco is burning," he continued. "I bought a lot of news printouts in town. We haven't been getting enough by radio. Fires are being set everywhere. Maybe uninfected people are sterilizing the city in the only way they can think of. Or maybe it's infected people crazy with their symptoms and the noise and smells and lights. L.A. is beginning to burn, too, and San Diego. In Phoenix, someone is blowing up houses and buildings. Three oil refineries went up in Texas. In Louisiana there's a group that has decided the disease was brought in by foreigners—so they're shooting anyone who seems a little odd to them. Mostly Asians, blacks, and browns."

She stared at him. He stared back expressionlessly.

"In New York, Seattle, Hong Kong, and Tokyo, doctors and nurses have been caught spreading the disease. The compulsion is at work already."

She thought of her father, then shook her head, not wanting to think of him. He had been so right, so wrong, and so utterly helpless.

"Everything will be chaos soon," Stephen said. "There have been outbreaks in Germany, England, France, Turkey, India, Korea, Nigeria, the Soviet Union. . . . It will be chaos. Then a new order. Hell, a new species. Jacob will win, you know. We'll help him. And Jacob thinks uninfected people smell like food."

"We'll have to help him to help ourselves," she said.

"We'll be obsolete, you and me."

"They'll be our children."

He lowered his eyes, looked at her belly where her pregnancy was beginning to show. "They'll be all we have," he said, "the two of us." There was a long pause. "I've lost everyone, too. Will you stay with me?"

She nodded solemnly and went to him. They held each other until they could no longer tell which of them was trembling.